The Burn Line

Adam McKim

"All men are created equal,
then a few become firefighters."
— Unknown

Chapter 1

The road twisted like a question nobody wanted to answer. Gravel crunched beneath the tires of the aging pickup as it climbed higher into the Pine Pass foothills, a steady rhythm broken only by the occasional jolt from a pothole. Jesse Brooks sat rigid in the passenger seat, his pack wedged awkwardly between his knees, one hand gripping the door handle like a lifeline.

Beside him, his mother stared at the road with the kind of focus that said she wasn't just driving—she was bracing. Her knuckles were white against the wheel, her jaw tight. She hadn't said anything since they'd passed the last gas station ten miles back.

"You sure about this?" she asked suddenly, her voice dry and tight like the air outside.

Jesse nodded but didn't look at her. "Yeah," he said.

"You don't have to go through with it, you know," she continued, her eyes still fixed ahead. "No one's making you."

"I want to," Jesse replied. He kept his tone level, but there was an edge underneath—something between determination and discomfort.

His mother scoffed quietly, shaking her head. "You think this is what he'd want? You think—"

"I'm not doing this for Dad," Jesse interrupted. His voice came out sharper than he intended. He glanced at her and then away, out the window. "Not really."

There was a pause. The truck rattled over a rut in the road, it's rusted frame groaning in protest.

"You remember what he used to say about fire?" she asked, her voice softer now.

Jesse blinked, eyes locked on the ridge line rising in the distance. "Yeah," he said. "I remember."

He didn't, not really. Not the way she meant. He remembered the way his dad's gear smelled after a long shift. The way he talked with his hands when he got excited. The look in his eyes when he sat too long staring at the flames in the fireplace, like he was seeing something Jesse couldn't.

The pickup rounded a bend, and a hand-painted sign came into view, nailed to the trunk of a crooked pine tree.

PINE PASS VOLUNTEER FIRE SERVICE – TRAINING GROUNDS

The red letters were sun-bleached and curling. A small flag hung limply beside it, barely fluttering in the stale afternoon heat.

His mother slowed as they pulled into a dirt clearing that served as a makeshift parking lot. A row of military-style canvas tents flapped half-heartedly in the breeze to the left. An extended green trailer sat at the back of the lot, with two brush trucks parked nearby— both sun-faded and scratched from what looked like years of hard work.

She turned off the engine. Silence settled around them, thick and immediate.

"I'll be back Friday," she said, resting her hands in her lap. "Unless you call before then."

"I won't call," Jesse said, reaching for the door handle.

"Don't be a hero, Jesse," she said quickly. Her voice cracked just slightly at the end. "You're sixteen."

"I know how old I am," he replied. He glanced at her, then softened his tone. "I'll be okay."

She reached out and touched his arm. Her hand was warm, a little shaky. "You don't have to do this to hold on to him."

"I'm not trying to hold on," Jesse said quietly. "I'm trying to figure out where I'm going."

His mother didn't respond right away. She just nodded once and let her hand fall away.

Jesse opened the door. Heat blasted in like a furnace. He grabbed his pack and slung it over his shoulder as he stepped out, boots crunching on the sunbaked gravel.

From across the lot, a man in a sweat-stained yellow shirt waved a clipboard and called out, "You Jesse Brooks?"

"Yeah," Jesse called back, raising a hand.

The man approached, his gait confident but relaxed. He looked to be in his forties, all lean muscle and tanned skin. His Nomex shirt was already dark with sweat at the armpits and collar, and he carried a helmet under one arm.

"I'm Chief Mallory," the man said. "You're the junior trainee?"

"Yes, sir," Jesse said, adjusting the strap of his pack.

4

Mallory handed him the clipboard without slowing down. "Initial here, here, and sign at the bottom. Says you acknowledge the risks, you're not gonna sue us if you twist your ankle or pass out from heatstroke."

Jesse took the pen and scrawled his name in the boxes. His handwriting came out smaller than usual.

"You ever done any wildland work before?" Mallory asked, peering over the top of his sunglasses.

"No, sir," Jesse replied. "But I've read a lot. Manuals. First-hand accounts. Watched some videos too."

"Videos don't carry hose line," Mallory said, but there was a flicker of amusement in his eyes. "Still, knowing your way around a Pulaski's better than not."

Jesse nodded, unsure whether that was approval or a warning.

Mallory gestured toward the tents. "Pick one that's empty. Keep your boots off inside. Dinner's at seventeen hundred. You're assigned to Riley's crew."

"Riley?" Jesse asked, eyebrows raising.

"You'll know him when you meet him," Mallory said, smirking. "He's the one that looks like someone shaved a grizzly bear and gave it a bad attitude."

Behind the trailer, someone snorted. A voice muttered, "Kid looks like he'd blow over in the backdraft."

Mallory turned his head sharply and barked, "Shut it, Turner. You weren't born with soot under your nails either."

The laughter cut off and Jesse felt his face flush. He shifted his pack again and tried to look like he hadn't heard.

"You'll be fine," Mallory said, clapping him on the shoulder. "Fire doesn't care how big you are. Just how fast you think."

"Yes, sir," Jesse said. His voice was steady, but his heart was hammering.

As he made his way toward the tents, the weight of his pack seemed to double. Every eye felt like it was following him. He kept his shoulders straight and his head up, even as the dust settled around his boots.

The inside of the tent smelled like sweat and canvas and something vaguely sour — the kind of smell that lived in old gym bags and damp socks. Jesse stood just inside the flap, squinting as his eyes adjusted to the dimness. Four cots lined the space, two on each side, each one with a thin mattress and a footlocker underneath. Only one of them was empty.

He dropped his pack beside it with a soft thump and exhaled slowly, letting some of the tension bleed out of his shoulders. His shirt clung to his back, already damp from the heat, and dust coated the laces of his boots.

A voice spoke from behind him — rough, low, and unimpressed. "Are you the junior?"

Jesse turned. The man standing in the doorway filled it like a piece of landscape that had decided to walk upright. He wore a soot-streaked yellow Nomex shirt with the sleeves rolled to his elbows, and his forearms were crisscrossed with old scars and faded tattoos. A fire helmet dangled loosely from his fingers. His eyes were pale and hard-set, and his beard looked like it had never heard of a razor.

"Yes, sir," Jesse said, straightening instinctively.

"Don't 'sir' me," the man said gruffly. "I work for a living."

"Yes… Okay," Jesse replied, fumbling. "I mean — okay."

The man stepped inside, tossing his helmet onto his cot with a practiced motion.

"I'm Riley," he said. "You're Brooks, right?"

"Yes," Jesse said, nodding. "Jesse Brooks."

Riley grunted. "Your dad was Jake Brooks. Volunteer out of Black Ridge. Died in that structure collapse six years back."

Jesse blinked, caught off guard. "Yes, sir," he said automatically, then corrected himself. "I mean — yeah. That's right."

Riley didn't say anything at first. He just looked at Jesse for a moment, long enough that Jesse had to fight the urge to shift his weight or look away. Finally, Riley gave another grunt.

"He was a solid hand," Riley said. "Didn't take shortcuts. Knew when to speak up and when to shut up."

"Thanks," Jesse said quietly. "I'm hoping to do right by him."

"You do right by the line," Riley said, reaching down to pull off his boots. "The rest'll take care of itself."

Jesse opened his mouth, then closed it again. He wasn't sure what to say to that.

Riley nodded toward the footlocker beside Jesse's cot. "You get issued gear yet?"

"Not yet," Jesse said. "Chief Mallory said after dinner."

"Good," Riley replied. He sat down on his cot with a creak and leaned back on his elbows. "We're cutting lines tonight. Simple stuff. Brush clearing, line widening. You'll get blisters, maybe a sunburn. Good first day."

"Sounds great," Jesse said, trying to sound confident.

"It's not supposed to sound great," Riley said, narrowing his eyes. "It's supposed to be work."

Jesse nodded quickly. "Right. I just meant — I'm ready for it."

"We'll see," Riley said. He reached under his cot and pulled out a canteen, taking a long drink before wiping his mouth on the back of his arm. "First fire you face down changes things. You come in thinking you're ready. Then you smell it. Hear it. Feel the way the wind changes and the ground begins to speak to you. It doesn't give a damn what you think."

"I know it's dangerous," Jesse said.

"I didn't say dangerous," Riley replied, leaning forward. "I said it changes things. Fire's not just heat and burn. It's movement, it's hunger, and out here, it's king. You don't fight it. You outthink it. You outwork it. Or it eats you alive."

Jesse's mouth went dry. He nodded, though something inside him twisted.

Riley stood again, grabbing a towel from the end of his cot. "You got fifteen minutes before the mess bell. The latrine's down the hill. You forget where that is, you'll be digging a cat hole with a broken stick."

"Got it," Jesse said, picking up his own towel.

Riley paused at the tent flap, then turned back to him.

"Your dad was a good man," Riley said. "He didn't let fear get in the way of doing his job. But he also didn't pretend it wasn't there."

Jesse met his eyes. "I'm not pretending."

Riley gave a slight nod — approval, maybe — then ducked outside without another word.

Jesse sat on the edge of his cot for a long minute after that, staring at the space where Riley had stood. The canvas walls whispered around him, rippling in the breeze. He wasn't pretending. But he wasn't sure yet what he was, either.

The mess bell sounded like someone beating a crowbar against a propane tank. It rang out sharp and sudden across the clearing, bouncing off the trees like a warning.

Jesse flinched, then stood quickly, brushing the dust from his pants. The air outside the tent was cooling a little, just barely, though the heat still clung to his skin. Camp had taken on a different rhythm since he'd arrived — more movement, more noise. People were trickling out of the tents, walking toward the mess trailer in small groups, some laughing, while others remained silent. Everyone seemed to know exactly where to go and what to do. Everyone except Jesse.

He followed the others, keeping a few paces behind. His boots scuffed the gravel path with every step. The trailer's hatch had been lifted into a makeshift serving window, and a man with a stained apron and forearms like split logs was ladling something thick and orange into dented metal bowls.

"Chili," the man grunted when Jesse reached the front of the line. "Or at least that's what we're calling it tonight."

"Yes, sir," Jesse said, taking the bowl carefully with both hands.

"You'll wanna eat fast," the man added. "Riley doesn't believe in digestion."

"Yes, sir," Jesse repeated, offering a faint smile.

"Name's Roy," the man said, jabbing a thumb into his own chest. "I cook. You don't like it, tough. You get seconds if you're breathing after training."

"Understood," Jesse said.

Roy grunted and waved him aside. "Next!"

Jesse turned and looked for an empty seat. Most of the fire crew had gathered around two long folding tables set up in the dirt. The laughter was louder now, the kind that came easily after a long day of sweat and sun. Some of the guys already had soot smudged across their faces. One of them — tall, broad-shouldered, with a thick tan line where his sunglasses had been — spotted Jesse hovering and waved lazily.

"You lost, Junior?" the man called.

Jesse shook his head. "No, just looking for a spot."

"There's one next to me," the man said, scooting down. "Unless you're afraid of loud eaters."

Jesse approached cautiously. "I'm not."

"That's what they all say," the man replied, shoveling a mouthful of chili into his mouth and slurping loudly. "Then they cry into their cornbread."

"I'll take my chances," Jesse said, sitting down.

"Name's Ortiz," the man said around another bite. "Engine crew. You'll probably hate us eventually, but we get the job done."

"I'm Jesse," Jesse replied. "Brooks."

Ortiz paused, then nodded. "Yeah. Heard about you. You're the one Mallory called 'legacy stock.'"

Jesse blinked. "Is that… good?"

Ortiz shrugged. "Depends on who you ask. Some folks think you're here because of your dad. Others think you're just here to prove something. Personally, I think you're either brave or stupid."

"Thanks," Jesse said dryly.

Ortiz grinned. "You'll fit in."

From a few seats down, someone spoke through a mouthful of bread. "He better. Riley doesn't like wasting time on dead weight."

Jesse turned toward the voice. A young woman — maybe a year or two older than him — sat with one boot propped on the bench, her elbows resting on her knees. Her blond hair was braided tightly and tucked under her cap. She looked like she hadn't smiled in a while.

"I'm not dead weight," Jesse said.

She tilted her head. "We'll see."

"Easy, Ash," Ortiz said with a chuckle. "You scared him off, and he hasn't even held a drip torch yet."

"I'm not scared," Jesse said, voice firmer now.

Ash leaned back and raised an eyebrow. "Good. Because fire doesn't care either way."

Ortiz nudged Jesse with his elbow. "She warms up eventually. Maybe."

Ash didn't respond.

Jesse focused on his food. The chili was hot, spicy, and surprisingly good. His stomach, which had been in knots all afternoon, finally seemed to recognize that it was allowed to eat. Around him, the noise of the camp buzzed like an engine coming to life — the clink of metal bowls, the scrape of boots, a distant bark of laughter from somewhere behind the gear trailer. It didn't feel like home. Not yet. But it felt like something.

Riley appeared from the shadows near the tent line, his voice cutting clean across the din.

"Gear up in ten," he called out. "Grab your helmets, sharpen your tools. We hit the lines at dusk."

The tables quieted almost immediately. Bowls clattered into bins. People stood and stretched. No one questioned it.

Ortiz stood with a groan and clapped Jesse on the shoulder. "Welcome to the deep end."

Jesse swallowed the last bite of chili and followed him into the fading light, heart thudding like a slow drum in his chest.

Chapter 2

The forest swallowed them whole. Dusk fell in layers, like smoke curling through the canopy. Shadows stretched between the trees, soft at first, then sharpened as the last of the light drained from the sky. Jesse followed the others single-file along a narrow footpath, the weight of his borrowed gear dragging at his shoulders.

His helmet sat awkwardly on his head, slightly too big. His Nomex shirt clung to him, the stiff fabric already damp with sweat. A Pulaski axe rested across his shoulder — heavier than it had seemed when he'd first picked it up. Every step kicked up a whisper of dust, the trail worn smooth by years of boots.

"Eyes up, Brooks," Riley called from the front of the line.

Jesse jerked his gaze forward. "Yes, sir," he said automatically, then winced. "I mean, yes."

Riley didn't look back. "This ain't a funeral march. Keep your head moving. You watch the terrain, watch your crew, and watch the wind. Every second."

"Yes," Jesse replied again, this time more confidently.

Ortiz, walking just ahead of him, turned his head slightly and muttered, "Don't worry. He barks at everyone."

Ash, a few paces behind, added coolly, "Except the fire. He respects that."

"Damn right I do," Riley said. His voice carried through the trees like a falling branch. "Fire doesn't lie."

They reached a break in the trail, a clearing where the underbrush grew thick. Brambles twisted between the trunks, deadfall tangled in patches of yellow grass. The edge of the forest looked untouched — wild, dry, indifferent. A perfect place for a fire to run wild.

"This is the perimeter," Riley announced, turning to face the group. "This line's been walked but not widened. We're gonna fix that. Cut ten feet deep from the trail edge, full scrape. No green left standing. Get the crap off the ground so it doesn't turn into tinder when the wind comes."

He pointed toward Jesse with the tip of his Pulaski. "Brooks, you're on scrape detail. Ortiz, take the ignition side. Ash, spot him."

Jesse shifted his grip on the tool. "Yes," he said.

Riley moved closer, eyes narrowing. "You ever swung one of those for more than ten minutes?"

Jesse shook his head. "No, but—"

"You're about to," Riley said flatly. "Watch your knees. Watch your back. Keep the blade low and move in clean strokes. You cut too shallow; the roots hold. You cut too deep, you waste time and energy. You'll find the rhythm."

"I'll get it," Jesse said.

"You'll get it or you'll get someone hurt," Riley said sharply. "And out here, there's not a lot of room for second chances."

Jesse felt his ears burning under the helmet. He nodded. "Understood."

Riley stepped back. "Light's fading. Let's move."

The crew fanned out in the clearing. Ortiz attacked the brush like he had a score to settle, grunting with each swing. Ash followed just behind, dragging cut branches clear of the line, eyes flicking constantly from tree to tree. Jesse picked a spot and raised the Pulaski. The handle felt rough in his hands. He brought it down.

The first strike bounced off a half-buried root, jarring his shoulders. He adjusted, reset his feet, and swung again. This time, the blade bit deeper, carving into the dry earth with a satisfying crunch. He exhaled sharply and swung again. Then again. And again.

The rhythm came slowly. Sweat poured down his temples and into his eyes. His arms began to ache. The muscles along his back and shoulders screamed for a break, but he kept going. Each stroke peeled back a little more ground cover, revealing the pale soil underneath. The sound of metal striking earth filled the air — a strange percussion that echoed through the trees.

"Not bad, Junior," Ortiz called from farther down the line. "Try not to fall in love with the dirt."

"I'll do my best," Jesse replied, out of breath.

Ash moved past him, dragging another pile of brush away from the scrape zone. She glanced at his progress, then nodded.

"You're clearing faster than I thought," Ash said. "Might be half-useful after all."

"Thanks," Jesse said, unsure if it was sarcasm. She didn't clarify.

Minutes became an hour. The sky darkened to a deep navy, and the air cooled slightly — not enough to help, just enough to notice. Insects buzzed through the brush. A distant owl called out, low and haunting.

Riley moved up and down the line like a ghost, offering corrections, occasionally stopping to demonstrate. He didn't praise, but he didn't complain either. That, Jesse was quickly learning, was the closest thing to approval he'd get tonight.

Eventually, the crew paused for a water break. Jesse leaned against a rock, panting, forearms trembling from the exertion. His shirt clung to him like wet canvas. Dirt streaked his face and arms. He could barely feel his hands.

Riley walked over and handed him a canteen. "How's the tool?"

"Feels like it's part of my skeleton now," Jesse said, managing a breathless smile.

Riley cracked the ghost of a grin. "Good. Means you're learning something."

Jesse took a long drink. The water was warm, but it tasted like survival.

"You feel that?" Riley asked suddenly, glancing toward the treetops.

Jesse frowned. "What?"

Riley raised his chin. "The shift."

A breeze stirred the leaves, faint but steady, brushing across the back of Jesse's neck.

"The wind," Jesse said softly.

"First lesson of fire," Riley said, his voice quiet but firm. "It always rides the wind. Learn to feel it before you hear it."

He turned away then, calling to the others, "Ten more minutes! Then we hike out!"

Jesse stared into the forest, eyes following the path of the breeze as it moved through the trees. The hair on his arms stood up. He didn't know why. Not yet. But something told him the wind would come back to that moment later.

* * *

By the time they made it back to camp, Jesse's legs felt like they belonged to someone else. The hike in had been hot. The hike out was worse. Every step home carried the weight of exhaustion, the echo of every swing, every scrape, every bruise blooming along the muscles in his back. His arms had gone from sore to numb to sore again. His boots felt like concrete. Nobody talked much on the return walk.

Ash led the group, a headlamp strapped across her brow, casting pale light ahead. Ortiz hummed tunelessly under his breath, just loud enough to be irritating. Riley brought up the rear, silent, eyes always scanning the treetops.

Jesse stumbled once, catching his toe on a rock. He caught himself before he went down, but no one said anything. No one offered a hand. And somehow, that felt right.

Camp was quiet when they returned. The generator had been turned off. Lanterns flickered near the trailer. A few figures moved between the tents — the rest of the crew either winding down or already asleep.

"Tools to the rack," Riley said as they reached the edge of the clearing. "Boots off at the tent. Debrief at oh-six-hundred. Sleep if you can."

"Yes, sir," Ortiz muttered, already unstrapping his helmet.

Ash didn't say a word. She peeled off toward the gear rack with practiced efficiency. Jesse hesitated, then followed. He returned his Pulaski to the rack, matching the others, then bent to unlace his boots. Dirt flaked off in chunks, revealing raw skin along his heels. He winced as he peeled the socks back and rolled them into a tight ball.

"You didn't pass out," Ortiz chirped, stepping beside him. "That's a win."

"I'll take it," Jesse said, his voice hoarse.

"Don't celebrate yet," Ortiz said. "You'll be lucky if your hands don't blister shut by morning."

"Looking forward to it," Jesse replied.

Ortiz grinned. "You'll be fine, Junior. Just keep showing up."

"Thanks," Jesse said, quieter now.

Ortiz gave him a casual slap on the shoulder and disappeared toward his tent, whistling under his breath.

Jesse stood there for a moment, the sounds of the forest settling around him — the chirp of insects, the sigh of trees in the dark, the low murmur of voices from the mess tent. He turned and made his way back to his own tent, each step an effort.

Inside, the space was dark, lit only by the faint silver spill of moonlight through the canvas. Jesse eased onto his cot with a long breath, the mattress creaking under him. His limbs buzzed, equal parts fatigue and adrenaline withdrawal. He stared up at the canvas above him. This wasn't what he'd expected. Not exactly. He had imagined fire, yes. And hard work. Sweat and dirt and pain. But he hadn't expected the quiet. Not the kind that came when the gear was stowed, when the jokes died down, when there was nothing left but the shape of your own breathing in a dark tent in the middle of nowhere.

He rolled onto his side and pulled the thin blanket up to his chest. Outside, the wind stirred again — soft, almost gentle — as if reminding him it hadn't gone far. Jesse closed his eyes. He didn't dream of fire. Not yet.

Chapter 3

Jesse woke to the smell of smoke, though nothing was burning yet. For a moment, he didn't know where he was. The canvas above him glowed faintly with pre-dawn light, and the dry rustle of wind outside carried the scent of pine, dust, and the ghost of old fire. His body ached in deep, unfamiliar ways — shoulders locked, calves tight, wrists sore from gripping the Pulaski too hard. A second later, he remembered. The tent. The training grounds. The line cutting. Riley's voice barking through the trees. And today — the burn.

He sat up slowly, wincing as his spine popped, and swung his legs over the side of the cot. The ground beneath his bare feet was cold, but the air was already warming. That strange mountain stillness clung to everything — no birdsong, no insects, just the quiet hush of heat waiting to rise.

Across the tent, Riley was awake. He stood near the entrance, half-dressed, rubbing his jaw with one hand and staring into the gap in the canvas. His helmet sat beside him, boots lined up with almost military precision.

"You're up," Riley said without turning.

"Yes," Jesse replied, his voice raspy with sleep.

"Good," Riley said. "Briefing in ten. Boots on."

Jesse nodded and began pulling on his socks, trying not to grunt with every movement. His fingers were clumsy with stiffness.

"Did it rain last night?" Jesse asked, reaching for his pants.

"Nope," Riley said. "Why?"

"Smells like steam," Jesse murmured.

Riley finally looked at him. His eyes were sharp even in the low light. "That's the land holding its breath."

Jesse blinked. "What does that mean?"

"You'll understand when it exhales," Riley said simply. He grabbed his shirt and ducked outside.

Jesse dressed quickly, his motions stiff and hurried. He splashed water on his face from his canteen, ran a hand through his hair, and shoved on his boots. By the time he stepped out of the tent, the sun was barely brushing the treetops.

The camp had transformed overnight. Where yesterday had been casual, even a little loose, this morning was all motion. Firefighters moved with urgency, helmets clipped, radios checked, gear slung into trucks. There was no laughter now. Just the metallic clink of tools and the low murmur of voices passing orders.

Ortiz stood near the gear shed, sipping from a battered thermos. He spotted Jesse and lifted it like a toast.

"Welcome back from the dead," Ortiz called.

"I'm not sure I ever left," Jesse said as he approached.

Ortiz chuckled. "You'll find out how alive you are once the line starts glowing."

"Can't wait," Jesse said dryly.

Riley appeared behind them, brushing past with a nod. "Briefing. Now."

They followed him across the clearing, where a half-circle had formed near the map board. Chief

Mallory stood at the center, arms crossed over his chest, a red bandana around his neck, and a coffee mug in his hand. Behind him, a large laminated map of the surrounding forest was pinned to a wooden easel, several sections outlined in red grease pencil.

Mallory raised his voice as the last of the crew gathered. "All right, listen up."

The murmurs faded immediately.

"Today's ignition zone is Section D — east slope, low elevation. Controlled perimeter burn; double containment lines have already been cut. The goal is to chew through surface fuel and push fire uphill in a controlled sweep. If we do it right, we stop it before it has a chance to feed."

Mallory gestured at the map. "We'll start ignition at 0900. Winds are projected to be light and steady, out of the west. Humidity's low. We've got water support standing by, and two brush rigs in position."

He paused, then glanced skyward.

"But I don't like the feel in the air this morning. It's dry. Still, watch for shifts. If you smell pine pitch or hear the wind change, say something. I don't care how new you are. Fire moves faster than ego."

Jesse swallowed hard. Around him, the crew nodded grimly.

Mallory looked down at his clipboard. "Riley's crew will run southern perimeter prep. You'll be reinforcing the old cut line and watching for heat breaks."

Riley nodded once. "Understood."

"Keep an eye on your junior," Mallory added. "Let's not turn him into a cautionary tale."

"I'll keep him close," Riley replied. His voice was unreadable.

Jesse stood a little straighter.

Mallory took a long sip from his mug. "Let's move. Boots up. Radio checks in ten. I want all gear staged and ready in fifteen."

The circle broke apart.

Jesse turned to Ortiz as they walked. "Is it always this quiet before a burn?"

Ortiz shook his head. "No. It's quiet when something's off."

"Off how?" Jesse asked.

Ortiz shrugged. "You'll know if the wind tells you. You'll really know if it doesn't."

Riley called over his shoulder, "Let's go, Brooks. You're on radio watch today."

Jesse blinked. "Radio?"

"You said you read the manuals," Riley said, tossing a handheld unit his way.

Jesse caught it, fumbling slightly. "I did."

"Then you're qualified," Riley said.

Ash passed them with her helmet under her arm. "Don't screw up the channels, new kid," she said. "Last person who did lost their eyebrows and their lunch."

"Noted," Jesse replied, double-checking the unit in his hand.

He slid it into his vest pocket and followed the crew toward the trucks. The sun was higher now, the light golden and dry. Birds had started to call again, but their songs felt thin and cautious. The land was still holding its breath. And Jesse wasn't sure he wanted to know what it meant when it finally let go.

* * *

The engine rumbled up the old fire road, bouncing hard over rocks and tree roots. Jesse clung to the steel frame in the back of the brush truck, wedged between Ortiz and a stack of line gear. The truck smelled like oil, pine dust, and sun-baked canvas. A red water tank sloshed behind them, strapped in with thick chains.

The forest on either side of the trail grew tighter the farther they went. Trees pressed in like an audience holding its breath, their trunks scorched black in places, scars from old burns that hadn't made the news. Somewhere behind the treeline, Jesse could hear the high rasp of cicadas starting up — shrill and nervous, like something was already stirring.

"See that ridge?" Ortiz asked, pointing ahead with a gloved hand. "We're setting up just below it. That's your work zone for the next couple hours."

Jesse followed his gaze. The slope ahead rose steep and rocky, with a few scattered trees and a lot of dry brush.

"What are we doing exactly?" Jesse asked.

"Clearing the edge," Ortiz said. "Widening the containment line, knocking down anything that might catch fire when ignition starts. You'll be pulling loose grass, cutting scrub, and trying not to faceplant in the process."

Jesse nodded. "Got it."

"You'll be fine," Ortiz added with a grin. "Unless the ticks get you first."

Jesse looked at him quickly. "Ticks?"

Ortiz shrugged. "They're the real hazard out here. Fire's dramatic, but ticks are sneaky bastards."

"Great," Jesse muttered.

The truck finally slowed and pulled off to the side of the road. Riley climbed out of the front cab before the engine even stopped. He unlatched the tailgate and barked, "Gear out. Let's go."

Jesse jumped down with the others, grabbing a tool pack and his Pulaski. The head of the tool was still slightly dulled from last night's cutting. He felt its weight settle across his palm like a challenge.

Riley pointed to the treeline. "You all know the drill. Section D's western edge. We cut low and fast, two feet in, two feet down. Jesse, you're on scrub pull with Ortiz. Stay in his shadow and do what he tells you."

"Yes," Jesse said.

"Save your energy for your work," Riley added. "And if you hear the ignition call, stop what you're doing and listen. Fire doesn't wait for stragglers."

"Yes," Jesse repeated, a little louder this time.

Riley gave a short nod and walked off toward Ash, who was already dragging a chainsaw toward a patch of fallen branches.

Ortiz tapped Jesse on the arm. "Come on. Let's make a line ugly enough to impress the boss."

They moved to a section where grass and dead brambles tangled between two stunted pines. The ground was uneven, crisscrossed with roots and loose rock. Jesse dropped to one knee and began yanking up the brittle grass, stuffing it into a canvas sack slung across his back. The sun pressed down harder with each passing minute.

Ortiz worked fast, clearing with swift, sure sweeps of his tool. "You ever wonder why they don't give rookies the good jobs?" he asked.

Jesse grunted as he pulled at a stubborn clump of roots. "Because they'd screw it up?"

Ortiz laughed. "Exactly. But also because grunt work teaches you what fire loves to eat. Once you understand that, you start thinking like it."

"Thinking like fire?" Jesse asked, pausing to wipe sweat from his brow.

Ortiz nodded. "Fire's lazy. It takes the path of least resistance. Dry grass, easy meal. Pine needles, dessert. Wind, now that's its ride."

Jesse glanced at the slope above them. "So, clearing this stuff slows it down?"

"Slows it," Ortiz said. "Redirects it. Sometimes, if you're lucky, stops it. But mostly? It buys you time."

Jesse went back to work. His hands were getting the rhythm now — pull, toss, reach, pull again. His knees ached, but his body had started to accept it. The fire line was beginning to take shape, a raw scar along the edge of the woods.

"How long have you been doing this?" Jesse asked, not looking up.

Ortiz scraped his tool into the dirt. "Six years. Started in the valley, ended up here."

"Why?" Jesse asked.

"Because I watched a friend lose his house and didn't want to watch another," Ortiz said. Then he added, "Also, I hate offices."

Jesse smiled faintly.

They worked in silence after that, side by side. The sky above them was bright and cloudless. The wind barely moved. It was the kind of heat that didn't burn so much as press — a weight on the chest, a hand on the back of the neck. Jesse felt the sweat soaking through his shirt, the sting of dust in his eyes. But beneath the exhaustion, something else was rising. Pride.

He was doing it. Not pretending, not watching, not shadowing. Working. Contributing. Clearing the line like the others. His muscles hurt, his hands were filthy, but it felt real.

Ortiz looked over and nodded once. "You're not bad, Junior. Could've fooled me."

"Thanks," Jesse said, straightening.

The wind shifted — barely — just enough to lift the hair on Jesse's arms. He looked up toward the trees. Nothing moved, but the air had changed.

"Feel that?" he asked.

Ortiz paused. "Yeah."

"What is it?" Jesse asked.

Ortiz didn't answer right away. He squinted at the sky and sniffed once.

"Not sure yet," Ortiz said slowly. "Could be nothing. Could be heat drawing air off the ridge."

"Should we tell Riley?" Jesse asked.

Ortiz shook his head. "If it turns into something, we'll know. If not, he'll chew you out for wasting his time."

Jesse looked back toward the line they'd cleared — rough, uneven, but clean. Exposed soil and stripped roots. A break. A barrier. A hope. The radio on Jesse's vest crackled once — a short, static pop. He froze.

Ortiz leaned over and tapped the device. "Test signal. Someone just keyed their mic on accident."

Jesse nodded, trying to slow his pulse. "Right."

Ortiz glanced back at the slope. "We're almost there. Let's finish the edge. Then maybe we get to stand still before everything starts burning."

Jesse bent down and went back to work, the Pulaski biting into the earth with a dull thunk. Sweat ran down his spine. Above them, the air remained still, and the trees waited, watching.

Chapter 4

By mid-morning, the heat was no longer something Jesse felt — it was something that *lived* with him. It clung to his back, filled his boots, crawled down the collar of his shirt, and soaked his skin. The sun was relentless, perched directly overhead, casting hard-edged shadows across the dirt. Even in the shade of the pine trees, the air shimmered.

He leaned on his Pulaski, breath heavy, watching dust settle over the scrape line they'd carved. Ortiz was a few yards down, hammering at a stubborn tangle of roots. Beyond them, the forest opened into a narrow slope of brush and low grass — the ignition zone. They were close now. Too close.

A shrill *crack* echoed up from the base of the ridge. It was followed by a long hiss — like air being let out of something deep in the belly of the forest.

Ortiz straightened slowly. "That's drip torch fire," he said, wiping his forehead with his sleeve. "They've started the line."

Jesse's stomach tightened.

"You okay, Junior?" Ortiz asked, eyeing him.

"Yeah," Jesse said, nodding. "I just… didn't think it would sound like that."

Ortiz smiled. "It never sounds the way you expect. Sometimes it doesn't sound at all — until it's too close."

Jesse looked past the trees. A thin line of smoke had begun to thread its way upward through the underbrush, curling like a question mark. It wasn't much yet — no roar, no glow—but it moved fast. He could already see the heat waves shimmering along the ground.

"Riley said to stay on the line until the second call," Jesse said, checking his radio.

Ortiz nodded. "He'll let us know if it gets too hungry."

Riley's voice came through the radio a second later, clipped and dry: "Team Bravo, hold the southern line. Eyes up, radios open. That fire's moving clean but quick."

Ortiz raised his eyebrows. "That was fast."

Jesse asked, "Should we move back?"

"No," Ortiz replied. "Not yet. That tone means it's not a threat… but he doesn't like what it's doing."

Jesse turned slowly in a circle. The slope behind them was clear. The crew trucks were parked a hundred yards back at the trailhead. But something about the air had changed.

It wasn't just hot. It was tight — like the inside of a balloon just before it bursts.

He swallowed and asked, "Does it always feel like this before a fire jumps?"

Ortiz's expression shifted. "Sometimes," he said. "And sometimes you don't feel anything at all. That's the part that messes with your head."

They stood there, quiet, as the smoke rose higher. Jesse could hear it now — the faint, dry crackle of flame licking over pine needles. It reminded him of the sound made by bubble wrap when someone twisted it slowly.

Suddenly, Riley's voice barked over the radio again — louder, faster this time. "Spot fire reported at grid echo-five. All units tighten flanks and scan the high ground. Bravo team, check your downwind."

Ortiz spun, looking toward the ridge. Jesse turned with him. The trees were still. But off to the right — maybe a hundred feet away — a curl of smoke was rising where none had been before.

"That wasn't there two minutes ago," Jesse said, pointing.

"No," Ortiz said grimly. "It wasn't."

A gust of wind pushed across Jesse's face. Not a breeze. A gust — sharp, sudden, dry as old paper. It carried a bitter tang that burned the back of his throat.

Jesse lifted his radio. "Bravo team to base. Spot confirmed downwind, southeast of current position. Smoke column active."

Riley's voice came back fast. "Copy that. You've got fire on the crawl. Get your asses back to staging."

Ortiz turned to Jesse. "You heard the man. Let's move."

They started downhill fast, not running, but close. Behind them, Jesse could hear the fire crackling louder now, no longer patient. Another gust of wind hit, this time stronger. It stirred the trees. Pine needles rained down in a brittle hiss.

"Something's changed," Jesse said breathlessly as they reached the trail.

"Yeah," Ortiz replied. "The fire just stood up."

They jogged past Ash, who was already tossing gear back into the bed of the truck. Her face was stone.

"Where's Riley?" Ortiz called out.

"Calling suppression," Ash replied, yanking the tailgate up. "He's ahead of us on the ridge."

"We need eyes on the slope," Ortiz said. "If it curls this way—"

"Then we're boxed in," Ash finished. She turned toward Jesse. "Get that radio up. Now."

Jesse's fingers trembled as he keyed the mic. "Bravo to Riley. Fire behavior is increasing. Wind shift confirmed. Awaiting orders."

The radio hissed with static. Nothing.

He tried again. "Bravo to Riley, do you copy?"

More static. A pop. Then Riley's voice came in, barely audible: "Hold line—backtrack—no—flank—"

The message cut off.

Ortiz swore under his breath. "We just lost him."

Jesse stared at the smoke crawling over the treetops. It was darker now. Closer.

"What do we do?" Jesse asked.

Ortiz looked at him. Then at Ash. Then at the fire.

"We fall back to the trucks," Ortiz said. "And we pray he's ahead of us."

The smoke wasn't drifting anymore. It was climbing. By the time Jesse and Ortiz reached the trucks, the thin columns of grey had thickened into a dense, rising sheet, pushing up through the treetops like it had somewhere to be. The wind had turned steady, pulsing from the south in sharp, dry bursts that carried heat and the sharp sting of pitch.

Ash stood at the tailgate, her radio pressed to her ear. Her mouth was tight, and her eyes kept flicking toward the slope like she expected something to come crashing down through the trees.

"No word from Riley," she muttered. "Signal is in and out. The spot's growing."

Ortiz dropped his gear and stepped beside her. "How far?"

"Too far to ignore," Ash replied. "Not far enough to escape."

Jesse stood just behind them, pulse thudding in his ears. The radio on his vest crackled with broken chatter — Mallory's voice, then static, then someone else shouting about containment loss.

Ortiz grabbed Jesse's shoulder. "Get to the cab. Radio back to base and request wind telemetry in real-time. Tell them we've got a spot fire running southeast toward Ridge Line Delta. Emphasize 'running.' Got that?"

"Yes," Jesse said quickly. "Running southeast. Ridge Line Delta."

He turned and ran to the passenger side of the nearest brush truck, climbed into the cab, and keyed the onboard radio.

"Base, this is Bravo Crew, over," Jesse said, his voice shaky. "Requesting immediate wind telemetry. Confirming active spot fire southeast Ridge Line Delta. Fire is running. Repeat — fire is running."

There was a pause, then static. Then Mallory's voice came through, clipped and tense.

"Copy that, Bravo. Wind has shifted ten degrees south. Gusts up to twenty. Repeat — gusts twenty-plus. Spot is expanding. All perimeter crews are to withdraw to fallback positions."

Jesse stared at the mic. "Fallback," he whispered.

Outside, Ash was already shouting. "Get the gear in! We're pulling back!"

Ortiz turned and called, "Where's the ignition crew?!"

"Still downhill!" Ash yelled, throwing a chainsaw into the bed of the truck. "We've got maybe five minutes before the slope cooks!"

Jesse climbed out of the truck and sprinted toward them. "Mallory confirmed wind shift. Up to twenty-mile gusts. He ordered a full perimeter fallback."

"Then we don't wait," Ortiz said. He pointed to Jesse. "Help Ash finish loading. Now."

Jesse ran to the other side of the truck, tossing gloves, helmets, and spare line tools into the back. The air smelled sharper now, not just smoke, but something rawer, more chemical, like the forest was waking up angry.

He paused and looked toward the slope. The fire was coming. Not the slow crawl of the drip torch burn, but a fast, low wall of flame rippling through the brush like it was tasting everything in its path. Orange tongues snapped at pine boughs. Smoke rolled low and thick. Trees shifted in the wind like they were trying to move out of the way.

Jesse felt his breath catch. This wasn't a controlled burn anymore. This was real.

Ash shouted, "We're loaded!"

Ortiz slapped the tailgate shut. "Where the hell is Riley?!"

Jesse turned, scanning the ridgeline, but saw nothing.

Ash keyed her radio again. "Riley, this is Bravo. Come in. We are in a fallback position. Trucks are loaded. Fire is moving fast. Do you copy?"

Only static.

Ash swore and dropped the radio to her side. "We wait thirty seconds," she said. "If he's not here, we leave."

"Can't just leave him," Ortiz said.

"We're not leaving him," Ash snapped. "We're not dying either."

Jesse took a step back, trying to take it all in — the smoke, the heat, the panic in Ash's voice, the hard edge in Ortiz's. Everything had changed in five minutes. The same calm trail they'd walked that morning now looked like the edge of a war zone.

The radio barked suddenly, distorted, but there.

"Bravo—Riley—coming in—north side—hold—"

Jesse grabbed the mic. "Riley, this is Jesse. We hear you. Confirm your location."

Static again.

Then: "North slope. Cutting through the old trench. Two minutes out. Hold fire rig."

Ortiz was already climbing into the truck. "He's coming in behind us. If he doesn't make it in two minutes, we roll slow and meet him up trail."

Ash took the wheel. "Everyone strap in. Jesse, take the passenger side. Keep that radio live."

Jesse scrambled in, slamming the door behind him. His hands shook as he held the mic. The truck engine coughed, then growled to life. In the side mirror, smoke blotted out most of the sky behind them.

Ash muttered, "Come on, Riley. Come on."

A shadow moved through the trees. Then Riley burst into view — helmet on, shirt dark with sweat, a pack slung over one arm, and a tool dragging from his left hand. He didn't slow.

Ash flung the door open. "Move!"

Riley climbed into the back like a man possessed, slamming the tailgate closed behind him. "Drive!"

The truck jolted forward as Ash hit the gas. They rolled fast over the rutted trail, smoke chasing them like a wave. Trees blurred past, and behind them, flame climbed the ridge.

Nobody spoke for a full minute. Then, as they reached a clearing and slowed just slightly, Jesse finally broke the silence. "The fire... it jumped."

Riley leaned forward over the seat. "No..." he said. He looked back at the fire behind them. "It ran."

Chapter 5

Jesse sat in the passenger seat of the brush truck as the tires bucked against the rocky trail, his hand gripping the dashboard like a lifeline. Ash drove with her jaw clenched and eyes locked ahead, knuckles white on the wheel. In the side mirror, smoke rolled behind them like a storm cloud chasing their tail. Riley shouted over the noise from the bed of the truck, his voice muffled but urgent.

"What'd he say?" Ash asked, glancing in the mirror.

"He said cut left at the split — north fire road," Jesse called back, struggling to hear the handheld radio over the engine noise.

Ash jerked the wheel hard. Gravel sprayed under the tires as the truck swerved into a narrow side path barely wide enough for the rig. Branches slapped the sides. The cab filled with a dry, resinous scent. Smoke threaded through the vents, sharp and dirty, clinging to the back of Jesse's throat.

"I thought this was a burn window," Jesse said, his voice tight.

Ash didn't take her eyes off the road. "It *was* a burn window."

"But now—" Jesse began.

"Now it's a runaway," she said flatly.

They barreled forward another fifty yards, then skidded to a stop in a clearing where the second brush truck had parked. Two other crew members — Ramirez and Dana — stood outside, one holding a shovel, the other adjusting a radio headset.

Riley jumped out of the truck bed and strode toward them.

"Report," Riley barked.

"Spot fires up the slope," Dana said, pointing. "Three visible flare-ups. One's already crowning the east side."

"Wind's not just shifting," Ramirez added. "It's feeding."

"Then we're out of time," Riley said.

He turned toward Ash. "Get water flowing to the lower edge and start soaking ground fuel. Dana, Ramirez — start a back-cut trench behind the rigs. Ortiz, check for any ignition crew still moving upslope."

"What about me?" Jesse asked quickly, stepping out of the cab.

Riley looked at him, eyes sharp. "You've got a radio. You're fast. I need you to run point down to Camp Station Charlie — tell them we're pulling from Section D and the wind's turned the whole slope hostile."

Jesse blinked. "You want me to go alone?"

"You said you wanted to be useful," Riley said. "This is it. Follow the road, take the left fork at the washout, and keep going until you see the marker tower. Can't miss it."

Jesse blinked. "But the smoke—"

"You'll get through," Riley said, his tone suddenly softer. "But you have to go now."

Jesse hesitated for only a second. Then he nodded. "Okay. I'm on it."

Riley clapped a hand on his shoulder. "Keep the radio live. Call out if you run into anything. Don't try to be a hero. Just get there."

Jesse turned and jogged back down the trail as the others scattered. Behind him, the forest groaned — a sound like trees bending and breaking in the distance, carried on a hot wind. He tightened the strap on his helmet and tucked the radio close to his chest.

The trail dipped steeply, winding between scorched pine trunks and thick underbrush. Smoke drifted low across the path, making the ground shimmer with heat mirage. Jesse kept moving, counting each breath. In. Out. Focus.

He glanced over his shoulder once. The trucks were already lost in the haze. He wiped the sweat from his brow with the back of his glove and turned his eyes on the trail.

"This is Jesse Brooks, Bravo Crew," he said into his radio, keeping his voice as calm as he could. "I'm en route to Camp Charlie. Wind shift confirmed. Spot fire has compromised Section D perimeter. Riley says the slope is hostile. Over."

Static.

He tried again. "Camp Charlie, do you copy? Over."

More static. A faint, garbled voice cut through for a second, then disappeared again. He slowed to a walk, then stopped altogether, listening. The only sound now was the wind moving through the branches. No birds. No voices. No footsteps behind him.

He looked around. The fire road forked ahead, just like Riley had said it would. One path veered left, narrowing into a downhill curve. The other continued straight, wider, but rising gently uphill.

"Left fork," Jesse muttered to himself. "Riley said take the left fork."

He hesitated, staring at both options. The smoke was thicker on the left. He could see the edge of a dry wash cutting across it, just like Riley described. But something felt... off. The trees leaned in too close. The smoke twisted in ways he didn't trust.

He keyed the mic again. "Requesting confirmation on Charlie station path. I've reached the fork. Visibility is falling. Repeat, visibility is falling. Do you copy?"

Still nothing.

He took a slow step toward the left fork, then paused again. The wind pushed against his cheek from the south. A pinecone rolled across the dirt.

He glanced down the straight path. Clearer. Brighter. Slightly uphill, but easier to follow.

"Maybe that's the one," he muttered.

He looked back toward the left fork — darker, quieter. He squinted.

Were those flames deep in the haze?

His pulse picked up. He made a decision.

"I'm taking the high road," Jesse said aloud, trying to convince himself.

He turned onto the straight path and began jogging again, lungs burning slightly with every inhale. Trees blurred past. His eyes watered. The trail curved. The smoke returned — thicker now, and sharper, carrying the sting of green sap and scorched leaves. Jesse coughed, stumbled, and pulled the collar of his shirt over his nose.

"Bravo to base, come in," he called again. "I need confirmation I'm still on the trail to Camp Charlie. Do you copy?"

No answer. Then, faintly — like a whisper coming from behind him — he thought he heard something. A voice. Calling his name. He stopped.

"Riley?" he called out. He turned in a slow circle. "Ortiz? Is that you?"

Nothing. Just wind, smoke, and trees that all looked the same. He fumbled for his compass, pulling it from his vest pocket with shaking fingers. The needle danced wildly. Then settled. He was heading northeast.

Northeast? That wasn't right.

He had gone the wrong direction.

"Damn it," he muttered.

He spun around, trying to retrace his steps — but the trail behind him was gone. The smoke had swallowed it whole.

"Okay," he said, forcing calm into his voice. "It's fine. Just retrace. Just—"

A sudden gust blasted through the trees, knocking ash into the air like dust from an old book. He dropped to a crouch, shielding his eyes. His radio buzzed in his ear.

"—Charlie post—unknown location—fire behavior —"

"Say again!" Jesse shouted into the mic. "Say again!"

The signal vanished. He stood slowly, heart pounding, surrounded by silence. No clear path. No trail markers. No answer. And the smoke was getting thicker.

"Okay," he said, trying to keep his voice steady. "Okay, okay… I went northeast. I just have to go back."

He turned and started jogging the way he thought he'd come. The trees closed in almost immediately. He ducked under a low branch, pushed through a curtain of dried grass, and stumbled over a fallen log he didn't remember. The smoke was thicker now, clinging to the ground in swirls, tasting of pine tar and old bark.

"This isn't right," he muttered.

He turned again. A flicker of orange glowed between the trees, maybe forty yards downslope. It wasn't big, but it was moving toward him.

He backed up, breathing harder now. He keyed the mic again. "Bravo to base, I have visual on active flame. Southeast slope. I am off the grid and reversing course. Repeat, reversing course—"

The radio cut off with a sharp burst of static. And then, behind him, something cracked like a rifle shot — a branch, splitting from the heat.

He turned and ran. He didn't think. Didn't check the compass. Didn't even know what direction he was going. He just moved through trees and brush, over rock and dry ground, chased by the growing roar of fire and the increasingly erratic rush of wind.

His pack bounced on his shoulders. His helmet slipped. Branches clawed at his arms and legs. He could feel the heat chasing him now — subtle, pulsing, insistent.

Somewhere behind him, the fire had found its rhythm. And he was in its way. He burst through a thicket, nearly losing his footing as he skidded down a slope of loose gravel. Smoke billowed from both sides. The world tilted. Every direction looked the same and none of them looked safe.

He dropped to his knees beside a boulder, trying to catch his breath. His hands shook as he fumbled for the radio again.

"Please," he said into the mic. "This is Jesse Brooks. Bravo Crew. I am lost. Repeat — I am lost. Fire is active in all directions. I need coordinates. I need—"

Static swallowed the rest. He lowered the mic, eyes stinging. For a moment, the only sound was his own breathing. Then he heard it. It wasn't the flame or the wind. A different sound. The high, eerie scream of something far away. A fox, maybe something else.

He let the radio rest on his thigh. Then he pulled out the emergency foil blanket from his pack and unfolded it with shaking fingers. The crinkling noise seemed too loud in the quiet. He draped it over his shoulders and leaned back against the stone.

He could see a gap in the trees. Just a small one, but enough to watch the light fade. The sky had turned from rust to violet, streaked with lingering smoke. Ash drifted through the air like snow, catching the fading sun and glowing gold. He pulled his legs close and rested his chin on his knees.

"I'm not dead," he whispered. No one answered.

A breeze stirred the grass nearby — cooler now, slipping between the trees with less purpose. He reached for his father's dog tag, which hung from a thin cord beneath his shirt, and closed his fingers around it.

"Guess this is the part where I start talking to myself," he said softly. He let out a dry laugh. "Or to you."

He paused.

"I tried to do what you did," he continued. "I followed orders. I worked hard. I didn't freeze when it got bad. But I still screwed it up. I lost the trail. I lost the crew."

His voice cracked just slightly.

"I don't know if I'm going to make it through the night. But I'm going to try. I just… I wish I knew what you'd do right now."

He leaned his head against the rock. Above him, the first stars blinked into existence. His body trembled, not from fear, but from fatigue. He was truly alone now. And somewhere far beyond the treeline, the fire kept moving.

Chapter 6

Jesse woke to silence. Not the comforting kind. Not the kind you get on Sunday mornings in a quiet house or beside a lake at sunrise. This was something else — a stillness so deep it seemed like the forest itself had stopped breathing.

He blinked up at the curve of rock above him. Morning light filtered through the trees in thin, golden streaks, cutting through the ash like theater spotlights. His body was stiff. Cold. Every joint felt locked, every muscle reluctant to move. He sat up slowly, the foil blanket slipping off his shoulders with a metallic crackle. His shirt clung to him with a clammy chill. A dull ache pulsed behind his eyes.

The fire was gone — at least for now. The smoke had thinned in the night, leaving behind a faint haze that drifted through the treetops like memory.

He checked his radio. Nothing. Still no signal. He exhaled slowly and pulled a small fold-out map from his vest pocket. It was creased and sweat-warped, the edges beginning to fray. He flattened it on the ground beside him and studied the lines, the red-marked zones, the trails.

"Okay," he said to himself, voice hoarse. "You came up the northeast fire road... then took the high fork... which was supposed to lead to Camp Charlie."

He frowned. "But it didn't."

He traced his finger across the map. "So if that fork was wrong, and I veered east..."

He pulled out his compass. The needle spun once, then settled: north.

"Then I should be... here?" he guessed aloud, tapping a spot on the edge of Section E — an unburned stretch of forest marked for future clearing, not current ops.

"That can't be right," Jesse muttered. "I didn't come that far..."

He looked around, hoping something would click. A trail marker. A boundary tape. Anything. Nothing.

Only the same endless trees and ash-covered earth.

"Maybe I should go west," he said, thinking out loud. "Backtrack. Try to find a high point. See if I can spot the ridge."

But as he stared at the terrain ahead — a steep incline, scattered boulders, dry underbrush — another voice crept in. The voice that sounded too much like Riley's.

The fire doesn't play fair. It doubles back. It tricks you.

Jesse stared at the map. His fingers tightened around it.

"Or maybe... the creek," he said.

He remembered spotting a dry streambed yesterday — shallow, winding, littered with leaves. It had to lead downhill. And downhill meant *somewhere*. Water sources usually ran toward access roads or lowland clearings.

"Follow the water," Jesse said, nodding to himself. "Water goes where people go."

He folded the map again and tucked it back into his vest. Then he stood — slowly, with a wince — and slung his pack over his shoulder.

Before he left, he looked up at the sky through the trees. The morning was bright, clear, and deceptively peaceful. Blue as glass. No wind. No fire. Just silence. He tightened the strap on his pack.

"Let's find the creek," he said.

His own voice startled him a little, too loud in the quiet. It sounded like it didn't belong. But he moved anyway, stepping out from beneath the rock ledge, each footfall muffled by ash and damp soil. The foil blanket he'd used rustled in his pack.

He headed west at first, angling slightly downhill, scanning the terrain for dips in the earth, for erosion, for stones smoothed by water. It didn't take long to find the streambed — a thin, dry gash in the forest floor, snaking between ferns and fallen branches. It hadn't held water in days, maybe weeks, but it was a path. And for now, that was enough.

Jesse crouched beside it, running his fingers through the gritty soil. "You'll lead somewhere," he said.

* * *

The creekbed twisted like a lazy snake through the trees, dry and silent. Jesse followed it with measured steps, his boots crunching over brittle leaves and bleached pebbles. The sun was higher now, filtering through the canopy in broken patches, warming the side of his face as he moved south — or what he still hoped was south.

He hadn't seen a trail marker in over an hour. Not a blaze on a tree, not a ribbon of flagging tape, not a tire track or boot print. Nothing but forest. He glanced down at the creek again. The banks had grown steeper, eroded from years of runoff. Roots curled from the soil in claw-like shapes. Occasionally, a log lay across the bed, half-rotted and covered in brittle moss.

"I should've hit something by now," He said, adjusting the weight of his pack on his shoulders.

His voice disappeared into the trees like it had never happened. He stopped walking and crouched down to study the map again. He unfolded it on his knee and tried to line up the curves of the creekbed with the terrain on paper.

But the forest didn't match. Every hollow looked like the last. Every bend curved just a little too far or not far enough.

"This has to be the same stream," he said, more to himself than anything else. "It's the only one near the perimeter…"

He rechecked his compass. The needle hesitated, then pointed southeast.

"I'm still heading the right way."

But even he could hear the doubt in his voice. A flicker of movement to his right made him freeze. He snapped his head toward it. Nothing. Just the branches moving in the wind — except there was no wind.

Jesse stood slowly, hand resting on the Pulaski strapped across his back.

"Hello?" he called.

No response. Just the whisper of ash falling from tree limbs, a faint pattering like dry rain.

He let out a slow breath. "Get a grip."

He pressed on. The creekbed narrowed slightly as it descended into a shallow ravine. The shade grew thicker here, the light dimmer, and the ground grew soft beneath his boots. Somewhere above him, a bird called once — a short, sharp chirp, then fell silent.

It had been nearly nine hours since he'd spoken to another person. Nine hours since anyone knew where he was.

"Ortiz would've said this was stupid," Jesse muttered.

He could almost hear Ortiz's voice: *"Creekbeds are good for water, not for hiking. You want flat, predictable ground when you're tired."*

Jesse shook his head. "Well, flat and predictable doesn't lead anywhere when you're lost."

He picked up his pace. But every step took more energy. The brush along the sides of the creekbed had grown thicker, thornier. He started ducking beneath low branches and stepping over downed logs. One slipped under his boot and nearly sent him tumbling — he caught himself on a rock with a grunt.

"Okay," Jesse said, panting. "Okay, this is fine. It's fine."

He stood still, listening. The forest no longer sounded quiet. It sounded empty. Like something had moved through and taken the sound with it. He took a sip from his canteen. Warm water, metallic and stale. There was only a third of it left. He capped it and moved on.

The creekbed rose sharply up a short slope, and Jesse followed it, using his hands to climb. At the top, the land flattened into a clearing — a small one, surrounded by crooked trees and thick grass. A good place to stop, maybe even rest.

But as he stepped into the clearing, he paused. The ground was black. Not charred. Just covered in a strange layer of soot-like powder. Not fresh, but not old either. He knelt and touched it. Ash. It had fallen here — maybe from a canopy burn, or from a distant column drifting in on the wind. Whatever it was, it made the entire clearing feel wrong. As if it had been watched by something. As if the forest had paused here, too.

He stood and turned slowly, scanning the treeline.

"Anyone?" he called.

His voice didn't echo. He stepped back to the edge of the clearing and sat on a stone.

"I don't know where I am," he said, staring at the dirt. "I don't know how far I've gone. I don't know if I'm going the right way."

He closed his eyes. "I might've made it worse."

He reached for the radio again, not expecting anything, but hoping.

"This is Jesse Brooks," he said quietly. "Still trying to locate Camp Charlie. I'm… unsure of position. Following a dry creekbed southeast. If anyone can hear me, please respond. Over."

The radio crackled. Then silence. Jesse stared at the forest for a long time. The sound of something dripping echoed faintly from somewhere ahead, like water striking stone. And for a moment, he imagined the forest exhaling again.

* * *

The terrain changed before Jesse noticed it. What had started as a slow descent through forest and brush became something harsher — the trees thinned, the air grew heavier, and the creekbed carved deeper into the earth like it had something to hide. The ground underfoot turned gritty and uneven, littered with stones sharp enough to catch the soles of his boots.

He'd stopped checking his compass. Stopped talking out loud. His body moved on autopilot now, one foot in front of the other, every muscle humming with the low ache of dehydration and overuse. His pack felt heavier with each passing minute. The radio bounced uselessly against his hip, silent since the last static that morning.

"Just another half mile," he muttered, his voice brittle. "Then I'll stop. I'll find a place to rest. Just a little farther."

But the sun was already starting to drop. He could feel it, even if he couldn't see it — the temperature shifting, the light turning thick and amber. Shadows stretched across the gully like reaching fingers. He glanced up at the sky through the trees and saw the color of old parchment — pale gold, tinged with smoke.

He paused beside a boulder and leaned against it, catching his breath.

"Where the hell am I?" he asked softly.

The forest didn't answer. He pulled out his map again — tattered now, streaked with dirt and creased beyond recognition. He unfolded it with stiff fingers and tried to line up what he'd seen with what was printed.

Nothing matched. Not the bend of the creek. Not the thinning trees. Not the steep gully or the jagged ridge rising faintly in the distance.

"I'm not on the map anymore," Jesse whispered.

He folded the paper and shoved it back into his vest, more roughly this time. He thought about turning back. But the way behind him was just as uncertain as the way ahead. No landmarks. No trail signs. No guarantees. And besides… it was too late. He looked around again, really looked, and felt it in his bones. He had gone too far.

The ground beneath his feet wasn't just unfamiliar — it was wrong. The trees leaned differently here, their branches twisted like arthritic hands. The wind had stopped completely. The ash was thicker, layered into the bark, ground into the soil like time had moved faster here. He wasn't just off-trail. He was off-route.

He sat down on a flat rock near the base of a dead pine, pulling off his helmet and letting it rest beside him. His hands trembled as he unscrewed his canteen and took a careful sip. The water was warm and nearly gone.

He wiped his mouth with the back of his arm and closed his eyes. He could hear his heartbeat in his ears.

"You did this," he scolded himself. "You picked the wrong fork. You second-guessed the compass. You followed a dry creek into a dead zone."

His voice was quieter now, almost numb. "You... got lost."

For a long while, he didn't move. He just sat there, staring at the fading light through the branches, feeling the ache settle into his bones. He pulled out his radio one more time and pressed the button.

"This is Jesse Brooks. Bravo Crew," he said quietly. "I am still alone. Still lost. I've followed a dry creekbed for miles. The sun's going down. I'm going to look for a place to bed down. If anyone hears this..." He paused. "...I'm still trying."

He released the button. No reply. He sat there for a few moments more, then stood up and began searching for flat ground, a windbreak, anything that could be a temporary camp. The night was coming. And it was coming fast.

After a few minutes, he found a hollow between two rocks. It wasn't much — a shallow dip in the forest floor, framed by a leaning fir and a downed log rotted halfway through. But the ground was mostly flat, sheltered from the wind, and free of obvious animal tracks. It would have to do.

He dropped his pack and sat down hard, stretching his legs with a groan. His thighs cramped almost immediately. His shoulders ached. He could barely unclench his fingers. He pulled the foil blanket from his pack again and spread it over the ground, then wrapped the edges around his legs as he sat with his back against the log.

He dug out a protein bar — the last full one — and chewed it slowly, forcing himself to eat. It tasted like chalk and salt. He chased it with two sips of water, then capped the canteen and set it beside his boot.

The air turned colder as the sun dropped below the treeline. The light drained from the forest fast — one moment the trees had edges, and the next they didn't. He wrapped the foil tighter around his shoulders, arms tucked close to his body.

He could hear things now — night sounds — but they weren't comforting. A branch cracking somewhere up the hill. A far-off rustle. The shrill cry of some bird slicing through the quiet. He told himself it was nothing. He told himself he wasn't afraid. He didn't believe either one.

He felt for the chain under his shirt again and held it like it might mean something out here. Then he looked up through the gap in the branches. A sliver of moon had risen. Pale and weak.

"I'm not done," he said.

It was barely more than a breath. He lay down on the blanket and curled onto his side, pulling his jacket close. The earth was cold. His body trembled from the weight of everything that had gone wrong. Eventually, his eyes drifted shut.

Chapter 7

The ridge rose like the back of a sleeping animal — steep, jagged, and indifferent. Jesse stared at it from the base, squinting against the morning haze. His knees ached just from looking at it. The slope wasn't tall by mountain standards, but it was long and uneven, studded with broken rock and clawed through by tree roots. His breath came out in a white puff, his first tangible reminder that the air had cooled overnight.

"One step at a time," he said.

His voice sounded foreign, hoarse, stripped down by smoke and silence. It didn't echo. He adjusted the straps on his pack and started the climb, boots slipping on loose pine needles. His legs burned immediately. He hadn't eaten since yesterday. His canteen had enough for a few sips, maybe less. His stomach was tight, but it wasn't hunger exactly — more like dread coiled up under his ribs.

Then something cracked in the brush behind him — a sharp, deliberate snap. He turned fast, eyes wide. His hand reaching back, hovering over the Pulaski strapped to his pack.

"Hello?" he called, voice louder than he meant.

The brush shifted. Then, from the shadows, something moved. His heart thudded against his ribs, loud enough that for a moment he couldn't hear anything else.

The brush thirty feet downslope shifted again — not wind, not branches swaying. Movement. Measured. Heavy. He crouched low, eyes scanning, every nerve pulled tight. Then he saw it. A shape. Mottled, gray-brown. Low to the ground. Coyote.

It stood still at the treeline, watching him with pale yellow eyes that didn't blink. Its ears twitched once. Its coat was thin but clean. It didn't look rabid. It didn't look afraid. It just looked... interested. Jesse didn't move.

"Easy," he whispered, raising his hands up.

The coyote took a step forward, nose low, tail down. Not aggressive, but curious. Jesse's mouth was dry. He reached again toward his pack, where the Pulaski was still lashed, and paused. The coyote tilted its head slightly. Then it stepped sideways, back into the shadows of the brush, silent as dust. Gone. Jesse waited. Ten seconds. Twenty. Then he stood, knees shaking slightly.

"Great," he muttered. "Now I'm lunch scouting."

He took off his pack and unfastened the Pulaski, gripping it tightly as he turned in a slow circle. The trees around him felt different now. They felt closer than before. He moved off the ridge, not down the same side he'd climbed, but skirting around it, trying to keep elevation, hoping to find a clearing, a road, anything that didn't look like another stretch of endless pine. But the shadows between the trunks thickened, and his steps grew heavier. The encounter had cracked something open in him. Something quiet, something buried beneath the resolve and the adrenaline.

He was no longer just tired. He was afraid. Not just of fire. Not just of animals. But of being forgotten.

They don't even know where you are.

The thought came uninvited.

They might've stopped looking already.

He walked faster. His boots stumbled over roots. He didn't care. The air was warmer now, and the wind had started to shift again — a dry pull from the east, like the forest exhaling toward him.

"I'm not gonna panic," he said. "I'm not gonna lose it."

He didn't believe it.

They told you not to leave the line.

He remembered that. He remembered Riley's voice — clipped, calm, always calm — saying, *Follow orders. Stay visible. Don't go off-trail unless told.*

And he had done all of it — right up until the moment when he hadn't. He stopped near a sun-bleached log and dropped his pack again, leaning against a boulder. His head was spinning. His vision swam.

"I just need to stop for a second," he said, but it came out like an apology.

He crouched down and covered his face with both hands, the Pulaski resting across his knees. The weight of everything hit him at once. Smoke. Fire. Ash. The dry scrape of wind through dead leaves. The coyote's stare. The cold silence on the other end of the radio. And underneath it all, the one thing he hadn't let himself think about.

This is what it must've felt like for Dad.

That thought landed like a stone in his chest. He opened his eyes and stared into the trees. The world swam in gray, green, and sunburnt brown. He could feel the pressure building behind his eyes.

Don't cry. Don't break. You can't.

But something inside him whispered: *It's already happening.*

He pulled off his helmet and let it roll onto the dirt. His body was shutting down. Not all at once, just slowly, like a battery draining it's charge. He picked up the radio again.

"This is Jesse Brooks," he said, voice thin. "Elevation increase... no signal. Still off-route. Still alone."

No reply. Not even static this time. He set the device down next to his leg. His eyes fluttered shut for a moment — not sleep, not rest, just off. That's when the memory hit.

He was eight years old. Sitting in the front seat of a truck that smelled like chain oil and burnt rubber. His dad's gear sat on the floor. The radio was on — real static, real fireground chatter. The sun beat down through the windshield. Jesse could barely see the station doors through the dust. He remembered how quiet his dad was. Not tired — something else. His hands were shaking. Just slightly. His voice had gone clipped and quiet.

"Jesse... if anything ever happens, you remember this: you stay calm. You get out. You breathe first. Then you think."

Jesse had nodded, but he hadn't really understood. Then the call came in. The speaker crackled. Something about a barn, a flare-up, and trapped crew. His dad flinched. Not visibly — just a tightening around his mouth. He never turned the key. He just sat there for a long moment, hands clenched on the wheel. Jesse remembered the silence. And the fear. Not fear of the fire. Fear of *him*. Fear of watching someone strong shake.

His eyes snapped open. His hands were trembling. He curled his fingers into fists and pressed them against the dirt, forcing breath into his lungs.

"I'm not him," he said. "I'm not him."

But the voice didn't sound convincing. His vision blurred, whether from tears or smoke, he didn't know. He wiped at his eyes with the back of his wrist and sat back on his heels.

"I get out," he repeated, more quietly. "I breathe. I think."

He closed his eyes again. Just for a moment. Just to breathe.

* * *

The sun was tipping westward again, spilling gold across the tops of the trees. Jesse sat in a crouch on the spine of a ridge, eyes fixed on the terrain below. He had scrambled up the last of the slope on hands and knees, the climb more desperation than plan, more instinct than strategy.

He had told himself that once he reached the top, he'd see something. A road. A tower. A fire crew. A reason to keep walking. But there was nothing. Only valleys and more ridges. The forest lay out in folding waves of green and black. No smoke columns. No tracks. No movement. Just an ocean of trees, stretching out beneath a sky smeared faintly with ash.

His radio was silent. He had tried it again twenty minutes ago, sitting under the branch of a wind-warped pine, pointing the antenna in every direction he could. He even climbed onto a boulder for height, waving it slowly, listening for anything. Nothing.

The higher he climbed, the smaller he felt. The wind had returned steady, coming from the north now, pulling smoke from somewhere he couldn't see. It carried the faint scent of something burned, something that didn't belong in the trees. Plastic. Or rubber. He didn't know if that meant danger or just distance.

He sat down with his back to the ridge and let the Pulaski rest in the dirt beside him. His fingers hung limp at his sides. The foil blanket rustled in his pack, but he didn't reach for it.

"I'm losing daylight," he said softly.

His voice barely stirred the air. He looked back at the sky, searching for any sign — birds, aircraft, even the blinking of a drone. Nothing. He imagined the crew back at camp. Ortiz chewing sunflower seeds, Ash sharpening her blade in silence. Riley hunched over the map board, barking orders. And no one saying his name over the radio.

Maybe they had assumed he'd made it to Camp Charlie. Maybe they were out searching in the wrong direction. Or maybe — and this was the thought that stuck — maybe they thought he was already dead. Jesse leaned forward, resting his elbows on his knees.

"I'm still here," he whispered. "I'm still trying."

The words no longer sounded brave. They just sounded tired. He stood slowly, wiping his palms on his pants. His legs wobbled, his back ached, and his feet burned from the inside out. He walked just a little farther along the ridge, toward a spot that looked flatter — a shelf of stone beneath a cluster of leaning pines. That would be camp tonight. He set down his gear, unrolled the blanket, and wedged himself against the rocks.

He didn't build anything. No fire. No shelter. He just sat still, staring up at the moon through twisted branches. He wouldn't sleep. He couldn't. Every time he closed his eyes, the darkness came alive — the crack of brush, the shriek of wind through high trees, the rustle of something not-quite-near and not-quite-far. His body throbbed with fatigue. His feet ached with every twitch. And somewhere beneath it all, his stomach cramped with hollow warning.

Still, he stayed awake. The fire was out there. He didn't know where. But the absence was worse than the noise. The silence made it feel like the fire had gone underground, waiting, circling.

He sat up just after midnight. His breath showed in the air, faint, like fog curling off a dying lake. The wind had picked up. It came from the west now, cold and dry. Jesse could feel it sliding along the back of his neck. And with it, the scent. Faint, but unmistakable. Smoke. His pulse jumped.

He stood, stiff and shivering, and scanned the ridgeline. He couldn't see fire, not yet. But the wind didn't lie. If it was carrying smoke now, it meant the burn had changed course. And it was coming his way. He crouched beside his pack and pulled out the Pulaski. His hands shook as he gripped it.

"I'm not going to just sit here," he said, teeth clenched. "I'm not going to let it find me asleep."

The silence didn't argue.

He found a stretch of brush twenty yards down the slope, shallow grass, a few scattered limbs, nothing too thick. If the fire came through here, it would move fast.

He ran his hand across the ground. Dry. Covered in debris. He started clearing it. One swing at a time. Scraping with the flat of the Pulaski, cutting with the axe blade when roots fought back. He made a narrow arc, then widened it. His muscles screamed almost immediately. His shoulder ached from carrying the pack, his wrists from the uneven terrain. But he didn't stop. This was something. This was action.

He dug a shallow trench, pushing dirt to one side. His breath came in grunts now. Sweat beaded across his brow despite the cold. The rhythm of movement began to dull the edge of his fear. Scrape. Swing. Clear. Breathe. After an hour, he had cut a rough half-moon in the slope, no more than six feet across, two feet wide. He knew it wasn't perfect. Not close. But it was his.

He sat down beside it and stared into the dark. His chest rose and fell in sharp bursts. His palms were torn, gloves worn thin. But his eyes stayed on the treeline.

"If you come," Jesse said quietly, "I'll be ready."

Chapter 8

By sunrise, Jesse couldn't feel his fingers. He sat hunched over the shallow line he'd scraped in the dirt, the Pulaski resting across his knees like a badge he no longer wanted to carry. He never slept. He couldn't. The firebreak stretched before him, jagged and uneven. A beginner's attempt. A scared kid's trench in the sand. The early light touched the tips of the trees as if it didn't know what had happened overnight. The wind had died sometime before dawn. It left behind a strange hush, like the world was waiting to see what he'd do next. He stared at the ground.

"What now?" he muttered.

His voice cracked. He hadn't spoken in hours. He glanced at his canteen. Three sips left — maybe two if he was smart. He didn't feel smart. His hands were raw through the gloves, his arms leaden. He had a scrape along his forearm from an unseen branch, a dull ache in his right knee, and a bruise forming under his ribs where he'd slipped trying to haul a log out of the line. But worse than all of that was the doubt. He looked down at the firebreak again and shook his head.

"This wouldn't hold anything," he said. He let the words sit there, then added, "Even I wouldn't stop here."

He stood slowly, knees clicking, and paced the line again, trying to see it through Riley's eyes. Riley would've torn it apart.

Too shallow. Not enough width. Poor wind barrier. No anchor point.

Ortiz would've made a joke. Called it something like *"The world's most tired squirrel hole."*

Jesse's mouth twisted, not quite a smile.

"You knew this was coming," he told himself. "The moment you lost the trail. You knew you'd screw something up."

He paused, looking around at the ridge, the hollowed trees, the brittle sky.

"You were just too proud to admit it."

His voice dropped lower now. "Just like he was."

The firebreak loomed before him again, like a monument to trying and failing. He dropped his pack at the edge and sat beside it. The silence pressed in. No radio calls. No helicopters. No boots on the trail. Just the creak of trees shifting in the morning air and the faint rustle of something too far away to care.

He leaned back against the dirt wall he'd dug and closed his eyes for a moment. The images came fast, uninvited.

Riley's hand clapping his shoulder: *You said you read the manuals. Then you're qualified.*

Ortiz calling over the hum of the truck: *You'll be fine, Junior. Just keep showing up.*

His mother in the cab, refusing to cry: *You don't have to do this to hold onto him.*

But he had done it. He had come here because of his father. Because the silence he'd lived in after the funeral was louder than fire ever could be.

"I wanted to prove something," he whispered.

He dug his heel into the dirt. "I just don't remember what."

He wandered from the firebreak in a haze — not a conscious choice, more like gravity pulling him toward shade and silence. His legs moved without thought, stumbling over roots, feet dragging through ash. He came across an overhang. The rock shelf was buried in the hillside, almost invisible until he nearly walked into it. A rough slab of stone jutting out from the slope, with just enough depth to duck under, just enough coverage to feel like a barrier between him and the world.

He dropped his gear and slid inside. It wasn't tall enough to stand in, but it was dry. The ground beneath it was packed hard and cool, and the walls cut off most of the wind. He curled into the farthest corner and wrapped the foil blanket around his shoulders. He was beyond cold now, beyond tired. The kind of tired that came from too much adrenaline and too little hope. He let his head rest against the stone. His eyes closed.

And then he was in the back seat of his dad's truck again. The old one. The blue Ford with the cracked dashboard and the burned-out dome light. The one that always smelled like sweat and pine resin. It was night, and the road outside the window rolled past in long gray streaks. The radio was on, but quiet — just static and breathing. He leaned forward between the seats.

"Dad?"

The man in the driver's seat didn't answer. He was staring straight ahead, hands clenched on the wheel.

Outside the windshield, flames licked the edge of the road.

Jesse's voice trembled. "Dad, I'm scared."

The man turned slowly, his face half in shadow. It wasn't quite his father. It looked like him. Sounded like him. But the eyes weren't right. They were tired. Hollow. The eyes of someone still stuck in a fire long after the smoke cleared.

He spoke in a voice like gravel. "Then you're paying attention."

Jesse swallowed. "What do I do?"

The man didn't blink. "You breathe," he said. "You listen. And you stay where the wind can find you."

"I'm trying," Jesse said.

The man reached for something on the dashboard — a folded map. But when Jesse looked down, it was blank. Just a white sheet. No lines. No trails. No roads. His father looked at him, sorrow in the corners of his mouth.

"You followed me," he said.

Jesse nodded.

"But I was lost, too," the man said.

And then the truck vanished.

Jesse jerked awake with a gasp, his heart hammering against his ribs. The air in the overhang was still. He sat up slowly, his neck aching from the angle he'd slept in. The dream clung to him like smoke. He could still feel the steering wheel, still hear the way the tires had hummed across asphalt. He rubbed his eyes. The sun was higher now. The light outside was pale and brittle. Jesse looked down at his hands.

"I'm still here," he whispered.

He reached for the Pulaski and laid it across his lap. This time, when he looked out into the trees, it wasn't just fear in his eyes—it was purpose. He closed his eyes again. He didn't want to. But he had to. And eventually, exhaustion pulled him under.

Chapter 9

Jesse woke to dim light and blinked into the half-dark, disoriented. For a moment, he couldn't tell what time it was, then he saw the pale sky beyond the trees.

Morning.

He shot upright. He'd been out for too long—way too long. Out here, with fire on the move, that wasn't sleep. It was a death sentence.

"You're going to die if you keep doing this," he muttered, his voice sharp with anger.

He sat up slowly, wincing as his joints stiffened and cracked. His muscles were tight, brittle, soaked in dried sweat beneath the foil blanket that clung to his skin. He crawled toward the edge of the overhang and pushed aside the curtain of branches and stopped. Ash was falling. Not snow-like, soft and drifting — this was finer, like dust shaken from old rafters. It danced in the dead air, clinging to leaves and bark, settling into every crack in the ground. There was no sun. The sky above the treetops was a flat dome of smoke, thick and unmoving. He stood, brushing ash from his arms, and stepped out into the open. The air felt wrong. As if someone had opened a door between dimensions and let the weather forget itself. He raised the radio. Tried it again.

"This is Jesse Brooks. Bravo Crew. Still alive. Still alone. Smoke cover is heavy. Ashfall started overnight. No movement in sight."

He paused. Then added quietly, "Please say someone's still out there."

Only the static answered him. He dropped his arm and stood for a moment, just watching the trees. He reached down, grabbed his pack and Pulaski, and turned slowly in a circle.

"I need to move," he muttered. "I can't stay here."

But move where?

He considered going west, following the ridgeline. It might lead to a break in the canopy. A clearing. A road. Anything. But part of him hesitated. If the fire was still moving through the valleys, the ridges might funnel it. If it came through under this sky, it would come fast. Still, standing here wasn't an option. He took one last glance up at the sky. And for the first time since getting lost, he felt a flicker of something cold and unfamiliar settle in his chest — not fear exactly. Not quite. Dread.

He moved like a ghost through the woods. He stuck close to the tree line, using the slope to his right as a reference, but every step felt uncertain. The world had lost its definition. Trees looked the same. Rocks looked the same. The forest had become a gray labyrinth filled with soft, falling ash. The last of his water was gone an hour ago. His mouth felt like sand. His head throbbed. But he kept walking. One step. Then another.

Then—A blur of hooves and fur and muscle crashing through the underbrush. Deer. A full herd. Sprinting. Not bounding — not graceful. Running. And behind them— Coyotes. A pair, maybe three. Low to the ground, long-legged, fast. Not chasing the deer. Running with them.

The ground began to shake. Jesse stumbled back, slamming into a tree as the stampede swept past him, a blur of heat and motion and noise. Twigs snapped like

gunfire. Ash exploded from the soil. The smell hit next
— smoke, thick and sharp. Fresh. Close. He could feel
it now. The subtle push of air — that sickening, pulsing
pressure that came before a flame front. The wildlife
weren't just running blindly. They were fleeing
something real.

"Fire," he whispered.

It wasn't a guess anymore. It was a fact. He turned
in a slow circle, trying to see through the trees. Nothing
yet. No glow. No roar. But he could feel it behind the
ridge. And it was coming. He looked in the direction the
animals had come from, then back the way they went.

"No choice," he muttered.

He gripped the Pulaski and followed the only logic
that made sense now. He ran with them.

* * *

The ground steamed. He stepped carefully between
the blackened trunks, each bootfall kicking up thin
clouds of gray ash. The smell was overwhelming —
sweet rot and scorched resin, like a thousand Christmas
trees gone to smoke. He was walking through a place
the fire had already claimed. The trees here were still
standing, but skeletal limbs bare, bark split, needles

reduced to a brittle carpet underfoot. In some places, the fire had crawled low, leaving only surface damage. In others, it had surged high, blackening the canopy and boiling sap out of the trunks. And it was silent. No birds. No insects. No trickle of wind. Just the faint creak of cooling wood and the hiss of moisture turning to vapor in pockets underground.

He kept his Pulaski in hand. It wasn't protection — not here—but it gave him something to grip. Something to focus on. He stopped at the base of a fallen tree, its interior still smoldering, a faint red line glowing along its core. He crouched and hovered a hand over the log — the heat was real, even hours after the flame had passed.

"Too close," he whispered.

He looked behind him, toward the direction he'd come. The fire was still back there — maybe a mile, maybe two — but it had been real enough to push the animals into a stampede. And it was still moving. This stretch of forest, though… this was a buffer. A gap. he stood and took a long, shaky breath.

"Good," he said, trying to believe it. "This buys time."

He kept moving, stepping over charred roots and ducking under sagging limbs. The air here was a little clearer because there was nothing left to burn. The forest didn't look alive anymore. It looked like memory. He passed a burned-out stump where something had dug into the soil — maybe a bear, maybe a human long before the fire ever came. There was no telling. The edges were melted smooth. The soil still warm beneath.

He glanced at the horizon, what little of it he could see through the canopy. The sky had not lightened. Even here, after the fire had passed, the smoke clung to the world like a ceiling pressed low over the trees. His stomach growled — a dull, painful knot. No food left. No water. Just motion.

He kept walking until he found the edge of the burn — a clear, sharp line where black turned back to brown. Where destruction ended and the untouched forest began again. He stood at that line for a long time. One step would take him back into danger. The other would take him deeper into uncertainty. He looked down at his boots.

"I don't even know which is worse anymore," he said.

* * *

By late afternoon, Jesse couldn't feel his feet. They moved, sure — they still obeyed him — but there was no longer any sense of contact between him and the ground. Just motion. Just ache. His calves had begun to cramp, sharp stabs that locked the muscle tight, then released without warning. His arms felt like they belonged to someone else. His stomach gave up protesting hours ago. Still, he walked. The smoke above hadn't lifted. Not once. It was as if the sun had been deleted, and the world was now lit by memory alone — a dull, oppressive gray that pressed on the shoulders like shame.

His boot caught on a hidden root, and he pitched forward, crashing to one knee. Pain jolted up his leg. He stayed there, both hands on the ground, Pulaski slipping from his fingers. His breath came in short, ragged bursts. He stared at the soil. It was cracked. Dry. Littered with dead needles and flakes of ash carried by the wind, he could no longer feel. His vision blurred.

"No water," Jesse muttered. "No food. No sign. No… no anything."

He slumped back onto the base of a tree and let his head rest against the bark. His fingers curled around the fabric of his pant leg. His lips were split. He had stopped sweating an hour ago — or maybe longer. The air tasted like chalk.

"I should stop," he whispered.

No one argued.

"I should just… stop. Sit. Wait."

Still, he didn't move. Because somewhere inside him — small, hidden, but still burning — something refused.

Not yet.

Jesse looked up through the thinning canopy. The sky didn't change. It never did. But it didn't scare him now. It just felt like another thing he had to move through. He closed his eyes and spoke softly.

"One more day," he said.

That was the deal. He would keep going for one more day.

Then they could argue.

Chapter 10

Jesse smelled it before he saw it — a sour, organic stench that cut through the smoke-dulled air like spoiled milk in summer heat. At first, he thought it might be an animal, maybe something dead and rotting beneath the brush. But as he moved closer, following the scent down a shallow incline between twisted pine trunks, he heard it: the faintest sound of water slapping against mud.

He dropped to one knee behind a deadfall and parted the branches. There, nestled in a sunless pocket of the forest, was a pool — wide, shallow, and greenish-brown. It might have once been a spring or a runoff basin, but now it was choked with algae, leaf rot, and stillness. Dragonflies skated across the surface, and the edges buzzed with small insects. The smell was more pungent here — not just decay, but something sulfurous and stagnant. Jesse swallowed hard, then licked his cracked lips. His tongue felt like burlap.

"It's disgusting," he muttered. "But it's water."

Cautiously, he approached the edge. The ground around the pool was soft and black, threatening to suck in his boots, but he crouched low and pulled out a small metal canister from his pack — the last thing Riley had handed him before deployment. A compact survival filter with a flip-out straw and a screw-on purifier.

"You said read the manual," Jesse said, his voice rasping. "I did."

He skimmed the top layer of algae back with a stick, watching bubbles rise from the murky bottom, then plunged the canister into the pool. The water swirled inside, thick and dark, but the filter held. He raised the straw to his lips and sucked. It was warm and earthy — not clean, not even close—but it didn't burn. And it didn't taste like death. He drank until his stomach ached, then stopped himself, panting, the straw still in his mouth.

"Okay," he said softly, sitting back on his heels. "Okay, that'll hold me. That gets me one more day."

He reached for his canteen and filled it carefully, trying not to stir the muck too much. The second bottle he sealed and stored in his pack without drinking. He'd ration it, even though every part of him wanted to drain it now.

He wiped his mouth and looked around the hollow. The forest here was twisted and close, like it had grown inward on itself. A birch tree leaned at an angle over the pool, its bark half-burned and curling at the edges like old paper. Everything here felt damp, but not alive. Like the forest was trying to heal from something it didn't understand. He stood slowly, rolling his shoulders.

"Back uphill," he said. "Back to the ridge. Find a clearer path."

He climbed slowly, his legs still stiff from the days of marching and cold sleep, but the water had changed something. His body was still fragile, but it responded now. The ache in his muscles had dulled from sharp to manageable, and his breath no longer came in ragged gasps. It wasn't recovery, not really — but it was survival.

The ridge rose in a wide arc, just steep enough to force a rhythm. He moved with his head down, boots sliding through the shallow dusting of ash that covered everything. Fallen needles crunched beneath his soles, brittle and dry, but the undergrowth here was thicker than before. There were ferns curled like fists, moss that had survived in the shade, and deadfall that hadn't burned. It meant the fire hadn't passed through this stretch. Not yet. That should have comforted him. It didn't.

The air still smelled of smoke — older now, filtered through trees and soil — but Jesse couldn't shake the tension in his shoulders. Something in the forest felt... changed. Not hostile. Not welcoming. Just wrong. He stopped at a break in the trees and spotted something near a small rock outcrop — a shape, small and slumped.

At first, he thought it was a fallen log. Then he saw the bones. Ribs. Charred and half-buried in ash. Whatever it had been was small — maybe a fox — its shape twisted, mid-run, mid-fall. The skull was cracked down the center. One leg was blackened to the joint.

His stomach turned. He didn't move for a long moment. Just stood there, staring. He'd seen photos in fire briefings — animals caught in brush burns, coyotes collapsed mid-run, owls with singed wings. But seeing it here — alone, silent, still warm with the memory of movement — made something in his chest go still.

"This is what it's doing," he said under his breath.

Not just burning trees. Not just scaring people. The fire was remapping the land. He stepped wide around the bones and moved on, the forest growing quieter again. Another hundred yards and he saw a second body — this one barely recognizable. Just a blackened mess of limbs and fur. Larger. A raccoon. The claws were still visible, curled like they were bracing for impact.

His throat tightened. He climbed higher, his pace slower now, scanning the ground. It was as if the farther he went, the more the forest began to confess what it had hidden. Burned feathers. Scattered hooves. A nest fused to a branch by melted sap.

"What didn't run fast enough?" he whispered.

There was no answer. Just the wind stirring faintly through the treetops, shaking loose more ash, soft as a sigh. At the ridge top, he found a clearing wide enough to see the valley beyond — still blanketed in gray, but gentler now. The smoke wasn't billowing anymore. It lay across the canopy like a veil. No flames in sight. No movement. Just scars.

He set down his pack and crouched beside a vast pine. His knees cracked loudly as he settled.

"I'm still moving," he said softly.

He sat in the clearing with his back against the pine. For the first time in days, his body didn't feel like it was actively failing him. He wasn't strong, not by any stretch. He still hadn't eaten, but he was stable. Hydrated, and most importantly, breathing.

"I might actually make it," he said quietly.

It didn't feel like hope, more like an observation.

He leaned his head back against the tree and let his eyes close for just a minute. His ears filled with the sound of wind in the pines, soft and high and constant. A breeze moved across his face. Cool. Clean. It stirred the leaves around his boots and brought with it the faintest sound.

A footstep. His eyes snapped open. He didn't move. Didn't breathe. Just listened. Another step. Not a branch falling. Not an animal crashing. A shift in the underbrush. Careful. Measured. Then silence. He reached slowly for the Pulaski. His fingers curled around the handle. His heart thudded once — a deep, cold punch inside his ribs. He stayed low, scanning the trees, holding still as he tried to pinpoint the sound.

Nothing. Then a rustle — not far. Maybe thirty feet away, behind a bend in the clearing. He rose to a crouch, shifting his weight silently.

"Hello?" he called.

No response.

His throat tightened. "If you can hear me… I'm not armed. I mean— I've got a tool, but I'm not looking for a fight."

Still nothing. He scanned the treeline for movement, for glinting eyes, for anything unnatural in the pattern of branches.

"Just wind," he whispered to himself. "Just wind and nerves."

But the wind didn't move like it had before. It circled, paused, shifted again — as if something out there was holding its breath. He didn't close his eyes this time. He sat still, watching the trees, as if the forest was staring back at him.

Chapter 11

The glint caught his eye first, not bright, but unnatural. Just a sliver of reflected light from somewhere between the trees, like sunlight on glass, only there was no sunlight. The smoke still lingered high in the sky, muting everything beneath it to shades of bronze and gray.

Jesse stopped mid-step, boots skidding slightly on dry soil. He crouched instinctively and narrowed his eyes, trying to make sense of what he was seeing. It was far off, maybe two hundred yards downhill, mostly obscured by the density of the forest. But the angles were too clean to be natural. Straight lines. A roof shape. Something solid tucked into the hillside. A building.

His heart kicked once, hard. He rose slowly to his feet, then jogged forward without thinking, adrenaline washing over the dull fatigue in his legs. As he moved, branches clawed at his sleeves, and the slope pulled harder on his knees, but he didn't care. It didn't matter that his limbs burned or that his lungs were raw from smoke and dust. There was a structure. That meant people. Radios. Shelter. Rescue.

"Come on," he breathed. "Please."

He crashed through a shallow ravine, leapt a fallen log, then scrambled up the opposite bank. The trees began to thin. The ground leveled. And then he saw it fully. It wasn't a cabin. It wasn't even a shack.

It was an old hunting blind — elevated on rusted poles, partially sunken on one side, the outer shell of plywood warped and peeling. One of the support braces had snapped, and the whole platform leaned precariously to the left. There was no door. Just a ladder missing half its rungs and a hatch above, half open.

He slowed to a walk, his boots crunching in the brittle weeds. His breath came fast now, but not from the run. From disappointment, rising hot behind his eyes.

"No," he muttered. "No, no, no…"

He stopped at the base of the blind and looked up. The thing had clearly been abandoned for years. Cobwebs draped the underside. Mold streaked the walls. A single sheet of tin had blown loose from the side and now flapped weakly in the wind.

"This isn't help," Jesse said, his voice thin and bitter.

He dropped to his knees in the dirt, one hand braced against the nearest support post. The metal was cold. Flaky. His fingers trembled. He wanted to scream. But he didn't. Instead, he just stared at the blind and felt the hope drain from his chest.

He didn't want to climb it. Every instinct told him it wasn't worth it — the way the whole blind leaned sideways like it had been struck by a windstorm, the way the ladder bowed, and the hatch creaked in the breeze. But even as his brain screamed to walk away, his hands were already reaching up, gripping the warped metal rails, testing for weight.

The ladder groaned beneath him as he hauled himself up, one rung at a time. Half the steps were gone or too rusted to trust, so he used the side rails, mainly pulling with his arms. At the third step, his boot slipped, and he nearly dropped. His heart slammed into his throat. He caught himself with a grunt, muscles burning, then pushed on. When he reached the top, he shoved the hatch open with the flat of his hand and dragged himself through. The inside of the blind was worse than he'd imagined.

The floor was soft in the center, water-rotted and sagging. One corner had caved slightly, leaving a dark triangle of open air where the platform had separated from the support. It smelled like mildew and rodent droppings — old life gone stale. Light filtered through slats in the wall, drawing pale beams across the broken-down hunting stool, a rusted thermos, and a plastic container with a lid chewed clean through.

No gear. No radio. No signal mirror, flare gun, dry rations, compass — nothing. Just the stink of time and failure. He stood in the middle of the space and turned a slow circle.

"That's it?" he asked the air.

His voice sounded too loud in the cramped room. He kicked the plastic container, sending it spinning into the far wall, where it cracked loudly and came to rest beside the thermos. The sound echoed once, then was swallowed by the woods below.

He crouched beside the small wooden stool and ran a hand across the cracked vinyl seat. The thing wobbled under his fingers, unsteady and useless, like everything else in here. He sat down anyway. It sagged under his weight but didn't collapse. He stared at the wall in front of him, not seeing it.

"You couldn't just leave a note?" he asked, voice quiet now. "A map? A name?"

He imagined the hunter who had built this thing. Maybe a decade ago. It could be longer. He'd nailed these boards together, climbed up here with a rifle and a cooler of beer, maybe. Sat here in silence, waiting for something to pass by. And then, eventually, he stopped coming.

He rubbed the heel of his hand over his eye and exhaled through his teeth.

"I ran for this," he muttered.

The frustration, the fatigue, the weight of all those miles suddenly pressed down on him at once. He hadn't realized how much he'd been counting on this — the blind, the structure, the idea of something being out here to prove he wasn't entirely forgotten. He wasn't even sure what gave out first — his breath or his voice. But in the next moment, his shoulders dropped. And he felt it — the first real break.

He didn't cry. Not at first. Just stillness. The kind that only comes when the body has nothing left to fight with. His hands lay open in his lap, palms raw and filthy. His breathing was shallow but even. His eyes stared straight ahead, but he saw nothing.

Eventually, he stood. The stool creaked beneath him as he shifted his weight, but he didn't care. He moved toward the hatch with the stiffness of someone far older than sixteen, lowered himself down the ladder rung by slow rung, and dropped the last few feet with a thud that sent dust and dry grass spinning.

The air had changed. Jesse felt it immediately — a pressure behind the trees, thick and damp. The first true wind in hours stirred the canopy. The leaves whispered above him like they were warning one another. The temperature had dropped slightly. The sky, already dim, had shifted another shade darker. Then came the sound. A low thunder rolling across the far ridgeline — deep and round, like distant drums on the other side of the world.

He looked up. A cloud wall stretched across the horizon, darker than smoke, heavier than ash. No lightning yet. Just the promise of rain, carried in the belly of the sky like a secret not ready to be told.

He stepped away from the blind and walked into the clearing, his shoulders hunched forward like he expected the weight of the air to push him down.

"This was supposed to mean something," he said quietly, staring up at the clouds. "Getting here. Finding this place."

Another roll of thunder moved over the trees. He clenched his jaw and felt his throat tighten.

"I thought I could keep going."

The words cracked at the edges.

His hands curled into fists, then unclenched just as fast.

"I thought if I just kept walking…"

He shook his head, and that was it. He sank to the ground, knees hitting dry grass, and folded forward. His shoulders trembled, his face pressed to the dirt, and the breath he pulled into his lungs came out sharp and stuttering. He let the tears come, silent and steady, as thunder moved again in the distance and the wind pulled softly at his shirt. The forest watched. And said nothing.

Chapter 12

The first flash came without sound — a sudden white bloom in the corner of Jesse's vision that lit up the forest like a camera flash. He froze mid-step on the slope, his foot catching on loose rock, heart leaping into his throat. The light disappeared just as quickly, replaced by the same heavy gray that had defined the past day. Then, ten seconds later, the thunder followed — deep and long, a slow-motion avalanche rolling across the sky.

He looked up, squinting through the canopy. The cloud cover had thickened. The air felt charged now, heavy with static and wet earth, like the atmosphere was holding its breath. He wiped the sweat from his temple and tasted salt. Everything around him was tense — the branches barely moved, the birds were gone, and the wind had changed again.

Another flash. This one sharper. Closer. Then the thunder cracked open like a fault line. He flinched, ducking low beside a mossy log, scanning the treetops.

"Keep moving," he told himself, standing. "Get to lower ground."

He turned downhill and broke into a jog, his boots sliding in loose debris, Pulaski bouncing on his back. The terrain narrowed as he descended, pinching into a low draw between ridges. He could already feel the temperature shift — cooler here, less wind — but not safe. The smell in the air was strange now, not just ozone or smoke, but something sharp. Coppery. Like heated metal.

As he moved through the corridor, the lightning flashed again — this time ahead of him. The light was brighter than before, so intense it turned the trees white and left a lingering ghost shape in his vision. He skidded to a stop, bracing against a trunk, and listened. This thunder didn't roll. It cracked.

A bird exploded from a nearby branch, wings flapping in panic. Jesse stepped forward slowly, scanning for anything out of place. And then he smelled it.

Smoke

"Damn it," he said, barely above a whisper.

He turned in a slow circle, trying to pinpoint the source, but the smoke wasn't thick yet. It was just there, rising like a question through the trees.

Another flash of lightning — farther this time — and another clap of thunder behind him. That was the moment it hit him: the fire behind him still burned, and now something had just lit ahead. He was standing between them.

He moved fast, his breath coming in shallow bursts as he pushed through a thicket of brush, branches raking his arms. The smell of smoke was stronger now. He couldn't see flames yet, but he didn't need to. The air told the truth before the forest ever did. He climbed a short ridge and dropped onto a flat bench of earth partially shaded by a leaning pine. The slope above him was steep, the one below even steeper — a bad spot for fire, a worse spot for water runoff, but the best he had within reach. He scanned the area quickly: loose dirt, rock cover, patchy ferns. No recent burn scars here yet. But the ash on the needles said they were coming.

"Gotta get low," Jesse muttered. "Gotta get under."

He shrugged off his pack and yanked out a crumpled tarp. The material crackled in his hands, stiff from days of use and sun exposure. One corner was torn where he'd snagged it on a branch two nights ago, but the rest would hold. He used the Pulaski to dig quick, shallow trenches on either side of a natural dip in the ground, then wedged one end of the tarp under a log and pinned the other side with rocks. It was sloppy. He didn't care.

"Not stopping the fire," he said as he worked. "Just buying seconds."

The wind picked up again — erratic now, gusting sideways, carrying smoke from both directions. He could feel it sneaking along the valley, wrapping around the base of trees. Somewhere to the northeast, a branch cracked like a rifle shot. He dropped to his knees and pulled armfuls of dirt across the lowest edge of the tarp, creating a seal, pressing it down with his fists. Every motion felt desperate.

His mind kept replaying Riley's instructions from the training brief: *"Shelter buys time. Nothing more. You need fuel, water, air, and an escape route. Shelter's the last line."*

"Not much of a line," Jesse muttered, sweat dripping into his eyes.

Once the tarp was anchored, he crawled beneath it and lay flat on his stomach, staring at the loose weave of the fabric above. His chest rose and fell fast, and his palms shook where they pressed against the packed soil. It was too hot to breathe comfortably now. The air under the tarp stifled, even without flame. It reeked of mildew, dirt, and himself.

Another flash of lightning lit the inside of the tarp like a bomb going off. The thunder followed instantly. He curled his arms around his head, forcing his breath to slow.

"Don't panic," he whispered. "Don't you dare panic."

Outside, the wind screamed through the trees again — a chaotic howl that didn't belong to the weather. Jesse closed his eyes, trying not to imagine flame fronts coming from both sides, meeting in the hollow like two jaws about to snap shut. He dug his fingers into the soil beside him and focused on the feeling of grit beneath his nails. It was the only real thing left.

The tarp fluttered above him like a flag caught in slow motion, rising and falling with each breath of the wind. The sound of the forest had changed again — no more thunder, no more lightning — just the low, unsettling roar that didn't come from above. It came from behind the trees.

Fire had a voice. Everyone in training said that. But nothing prepared him for the sound of it when it wasn't distant or controlled. This wasn't the hiss of backburn lines or the pop of flashover. It was a growl — low, steady, and growing louder with every passing minute. And it was coming from two directions.

The roar deepened — no longer distant, but pressed tight against the edges of the hollow like a wave about to break. Jesse curled tighter under the tarp, face to the ground, breath caught in his throat. The air rippled with heat, thick and pulsing, and above him, the fabric began to glow. Flickers of orange bled through the weave like blood through gauze.

The sound changed. It wasn't just wind and branches anymore. It was movement — force — rushing low and fast, like a tidal current through the trees. He could hear the crack of trunks splitting, the pop of pitch igniting, the sharp hiss of moisture boiling out of sapwood.

The heat spiked. The ground beneath his chest grew hot enough to sting through his shirt. Smoke pushed in under the tarp, swirling in long, searching fingers. It didn't come all at once, but in pulses — like the fire was breathing. Every few seconds, the air shifted, thicker, hotter, more aggressive.

Jesse pressed his mouth to the dirt and tried not to cough. His eyes stung. His palms burned where they gripped the soil. Sweat ran from his scalp into his ears, and his legs trembled uncontrollably.

He couldn't hear anything else now — just the fire. The tarp flapped once, caught by a gust, then slammed back down. Sparks peppered the edges — not close enough to burn through, but close enough to see the glow.

Time unraveled. One minute. Two. Maybe five. It felt like hours. The heat pressed in, blistering and endless. Jesse clenched his jaw and dug his fingers deeper into the dirt. Focused on that. Not the fire. Not the air. Not the sound of something vast and merciless slipping past just feet away.

Then, as suddenly as it had come, the pitch began to drop. The sound softened. Just a little. The heat broke — not gone, but eased, like a fever falling a single degree. The smoke no longer surged in waves. It drifted. Lingered. The soil beneath him still burned with memory, but the ground wasn't trembling anymore.

He stayed where he was. Listening. Another minute passed. Then another. No more flapping tarp. No more embers in the corners of his vision. Just the afterimage — a red glow burned into his mind even with his eyes closed. He didn't move. He couldn't. His body had gone stiff with fear and heat. His jaw ached. His ribs hurt from breathing shallow.

Then — a breath. Cooler. Just barely. But real. He opened his eyes. The inside of the tarp was dark now. Smoke pooled beneath it like mist on a river. He rolled to his side and peeked beneath the edge. He didn't know if it was over. But the fire had moved. And somehow, he was still alive.

Chapter 13

The creek bed was bone dry, but Jesse crouched in it anyway, using the heel of his boot to scrape at the earth, revealing layers of crumbled ash and old sediment baked hard by sun and fire. The soil underneath was pale and cracked like burnt skin. Nothing living remained. He scanned the banks for anything — a trickle, a pool, even mud — but there was nothing. Just rock and memory.

Still, he didn't give up. He followed the dry ribbon of the creek until he found a pocket of soot-covered gravel shaded by fallen branches. There, tucked into the curve of a boulder, was a shallow indentation no deeper than a soup bowl, lined with blackened bits of bark and moss.

Inside was water. It had a green sheen and was still as glass, but he crouched beside it like a priest at an altar. He unscrewed the lid of his canteen, swished out the last half-ounce of stale liquid, and dug into his pack for a piece of charcoal he'd salvaged from a burned pine trunk the day before. It had split clean from the bark like a wedge of slate, and he had wrapped it in a torn corner of his foil blanket like a relic.

He crushed it between two stones, breaking it down into a fine black dust, then dropped a pinch into the pool. The water darkened immediately, swirling with oily threads of charcoal. He stirred it with a stick, letting it settle, then filtered it slowly through his survival straw into the canteen, mouth tight, hands steady.

"Black teeth," he muttered, watching the liquid dribble. "That's what they used to call it, right? Fire teeth?"

No one answered. He took a sip. The water was gritty, bitter, and warm — but it didn't burn. No stomach cramps. No vomit. That meant it would do. He took another, then sat back and closed his eyes for a moment, the breeze moving across his face like something half-remembered.

"Okay," he said to himself. "You've got fluids. That's one thing."

He looked around the dry bed, scanning the trees. The sun — or whatever light passed for it these days — filtered down weakly, making everything look sepia-toned and old.

"This place is still burning," Jesse murmured, as if reminding himself. "Even if you can't see the flames."

He pulled the charcoal fragment from his pack again and pocketed a smaller shard in his shirt. Not for water. For signal. If the smoke thickened again, he could draw arrows on rocks. If someone passed through after him, they might see the black mark and follow. It was primitive. But everything he was doing now was.

He took another sip of the water and whispered, "You're not dying today." Then he capped the canteen, stood, and moved on.

The forest was quieter than it had any right to be. He moved through it like a shadow — slow, steady, deliberate. The trees were thin here, the ground dry, the underbrush choked with ferns curling in on themselves. Somewhere overhead, a crow called once, then stopped. Even the insects had gone sparse. The fire had swept through days ago, but the memory of heat still clung to the trunks like grease.

He stepped over a rotting log and paused to catch his breath. His legs didn't hurt the way they used to — they just felt distant, like they belonged to someone else. His fingers were numb around the Pulaski handle. He hadn't eaten since yesterday morning. Just charcoal water and three acorns he'd chewed until his jaw locked up.

He chuckled once — just air, no real humor. "You'd hate this," he muttered. "You'd call it a character builder."

He was talking to Riley now, or maybe to his dad. He wasn't sure which. The line between them had blurred a while ago — one barked orders, the other gave quiet warnings. Both had left him.

"You'd say I should've paid more attention during compass drills. Should've eaten more. Slept more. Shut up and listened."

He stepped onto a patch of moss that sank beneath his boot and adjusted the Pulaski on his shoulder. The weight of it had become part of him now. An extension. Not just a tool — a presence. He kept walking. Every now and then, he'd say something — a phrase, a comment, a joke only he understood.

"Did you see that squirrel? No? Yeah, me neither."

Or, "If this were a video game, there'd be a glowing trail by now."

Or just, "Still here. Still walking. Still me."

He wasn't sure why he said it. Maybe it was to remind the forest. Maybe it was to remind himself. The sun stayed muted above the smoke layer, a dull orb hidden behind colorless haze. It could've been morning or late afternoon — time had become untethered. He passed a tree with a split trunk and whispered, "That one looks like it's screaming."

Then he laughed. A quiet sound. Not mad. Not yet. Just tired. So tired. He stopped beneath a leaning birch and sat on the ground, pulling his knees up and resting his arms across them. His head hung forward. The Pulaski sat across his boots like a relic.

"Maybe I'll just... close my eyes," he murmured. And then, louder, to the empty trees, "You're not allowed to eat me until I'm all the way dead. That's the rule."

The wind didn't answer. But something else did — far off, low, carried on the shifting air like a growl from memory. He looked up slowly. His mouth went dry again.

"That wasn't thunder," he whispered.

He waited, breath caught halfway in his throat, head tilted toward the trees. Nothing moved. No wind. No birdsong. Just the forest holding still the way it sometimes did before something changed — before a limb cracked, or a fire popped, or the silence finally gave up what it had been hiding.

He stared into the trees where the sound had come from. He hadn't imagined it. His ears were too sharp now, tuned by days of solitude, sharpened by hours of walking without music or machines. That wasn't thunder. That wasn't a falling tree or a trick of air. It had come low — almost guttural — like an exhale dragged across a dry throat. Something alive. Or once alive.

He stood slowly, trying not to disturb the pine needles beneath his boots. The Pulaski felt heavier now, as if the weight of it had taken on a different meaning than it had just minutes ago. He turned in a slow circle, scanning the trees, eyes tracking every branch and shadow. Then it came again. Closer. His heart kicked hard once in his chest.

"Okay," he whispered, gripping the tool tightly. "Okay. We're not waiting to find out."

He didn't run. He couldn't. But he moved east — he thought — down a narrow slope of soft earth and fallen limbs. The air here smelled older, thicker, like damp caves and wet moss. Every few steps, he paused, listening. Every time he stopped, the silence around him felt more expectant.

He didn't speak anymore. Whatever part of him had needed to hear his own voice had gone quiet. The trees thinned slightly, and he picked up his pace. Whatever was behind him — real or imagined — wasn't going to wait forever. He passed a stump blackened by old flame, its hollow filled with water like a shallow mouth, and ducked low behind it for cover. No movement followed. No sound. But he felt eyes on him. Felt breath behind the leaves. His legs itched to move again.

He took one slow breath and whispered to the forest. "I heard you."

Chapter 14

The air was quiet again — unnaturally so. Even the wind seemed to be holding back. Smoke still lingered in the upper branches, but here in the hollow, the world had settled into that strange post-burn hush. It was hard to tell what had lived, what had fled, and what might be watching.

"I'm not food," Jesse said, as if that would settle it.

He set down his pack beneath a half-fallen tree, where the roots had upended a slope of dirt and tangled vines. It wasn't shelter, not really — but it gave him one side protected. Three directions to monitor was better than four.

"I'll move again tomorrow," he muttered. "Just need to rest the legs. Let the smoke clear."

The truth was, he didn't want to move deeper tonight. The trail was beginning to mess with him. The farther he went, the more he felt like he was following something that wanted to be followed.

He pulled out his tarp and pinned one corner across the open root system, tucking it low to the ground. It would break the wind, not much else. Then he turned to the alarm.

He found two narrow trees about ten feet apart and tied a line between them using what was left of his paracord. Then he strung the empty aluminum can from his water filter to the center, adding two gravel chunks inside to muffle the noise. A tug on the cord would shake the can enough to wake him. He tested it. The can clinked. Good enough. He sat back against the roots and rubbed his eyes.

"I swear," he muttered, "if this turns out to be some raccoon with a limp, I'm gonna lose it."

Still, he kept the Pulaski within reach. Still, he layered ash across the front of his tarp to help hide it. Still, he watched the treeline until his eyelids betrayed him and began to drift closed.

The last thing he heard before sleep took him was the slow creak of branches overhead and the faintest shuffle in the leaves. Then the dream began.

He was running barefoot, no gear, through a corridor of trees that leaned in too close, their branches clawing at his shoulders, their bark warm like breathing skin. Smoke clung to the ground like mist, and each step sent it swirling. His feet landed on coal, but it didn't burn. Not at first. Behind him, there was a sound. A rasping growl that vibrated through the roots of the forest itself.

He kept running, lungs aching, hands out to push the trees aside, but the forest gave him no room. The path narrowed. The ground cracked. He stumbled, and when he hit the dirt, it was soft and hot, like landing on the edge of a fire pit.

He turned. And saw eyes in the dark. They blinked once and moved forward. He couldn't scream. His throat locked. The fire returned all at once, roaring through the branches like breath from a god. The flames didn't spread. They leapt. He threw his arms up, but it was no use. The heat hit him like a punch to the chest, and the last thing he heard in the dream wasn't the fire, or the animal, or the forest cracking.

It was his father's voice. "You waited too long."

Then something snapped. Not in the dream, but outside, in the absolute dark, close enough to make his eyes shoot open and his breath catch mid-inhale. The pop of a twig under weight. Deliberate. Followed by the soft crunch of ash and needles being displaced.

He didn't move at first. Just listened. One heartbeat. Two. The can alarm hadn't gone off. But something was out there. He slid a hand toward the Pulaski, fingers closing around the handle like it had always belonged to him. His legs were stiff, sore from sleep, and cold, but they remembered what to do. He eased himself upright without a sound, crouched beneath the low tarp wall, and tilted his head toward the sound.

Another step. He could feel it more than hear it now, a pressure in the air, like the forest was making room for something big. Not a deer. Too slow. Not a person. Too heavy. The steps had rhythm. A confidence. His stomach dropped.

Bear. The word didn't feel like a guess. It felt like a confirmation. He swallowed hard and fought the urge to run. Movement would trigger pursuit. Every fire training manual said so. If you surprised a black bear at night, you didn't bolt. You made yourself look big. You gave it space. You didn't scream — unless you had to. His fingers tightened around the Pulaski. His other hand moved to his pocket. The lighter. He hadn't used it in over a day. Fuel was low. But it only needed to spark once.

Another step. Closer. Now he could hear breath, short, thick exhales, almost huffs. The sound of something sniffing the air. Then the rasp of claws on bark. It was right there. He pulled the tarp open, just enough to look out and froze.

Ten feet away, a massive shape loomed between two trees. Low to the ground. Muscular. Its back rose and fell like a bellows. A pair of eyes reflected faint moonlight. They blinked. The creature snorted once and stepped forward — a heavy, padded foot landing square in the dirt. Jesse acted without thinking. He flicked the lighter once, twice — click-click — and it caught. The tiny flame wavered in the wind, but it held.

"Hey!" he barked.

His voice was sharp. Clear. The bear stopped. Jesse didn't wait. He grabbed a fistful of dry moss from the edge of his tarp, held it in the flame, and watched it catch. It flared yellow, then orange, then started to smoke. He hurled it toward the animal's feet. It landed short — just smoke, barely a flame — but the bear reared back slightly, pawed at the ground, then turned.

For three seconds, Jesse couldn't breathe. Then the bear bolted, a fast retreat into shadow. Gone. Just like that.

Jesse stood in the glow of the dying moss, his chest heaving, the Pulaski still clutched in one hand and the lighter burning out in the other.

"Holy hell," he whispered.

But even that felt like an understatement. He didn't sit down right away. He just stood there in the semi-dark. His chest rose and fell too fast, too shallow. His ribs felt like a cage barely containing the thing inside him — a sudden, hot, electric understanding.

That wasn't panic he'd felt. It had been action. Raw and unthinking. He hadn't screamed. He hadn't run. He'd done what he needed to do, and the thing had backed off. He was still alive.

He crouched and ran his hand through the dirt where the moss had burned out, smearing the last of the soot across his fingers. He looked up at the path the bear had taken, but there was nothing now. No movement. No sound. The adrenaline drained slowly.

"I should be shaking," he whispered.

But he wasn't. Not yet. His muscles were tight, locked in, like his whole body had forgotten how to relax. He closed his eyes and leaned back against the root wall behind him, breathing deeply. The ash smell had been replaced by something sharper — sweat, ozone, the lingering scent of singed moss, and the thick, animal musk the bear had left behind. He opened his canteen and drank slowly. The water tasted worse than it had earlier. But he forced himself to swallow it.

"I could've died," he said. "That was real."

The words felt strange. Not scary. Not sad. Just true. He looked at the lighter in his hand. The metal was still warm. He set it down gently beside his knee and wiped his palm on his pant leg. That animal hadn't been curious. It was hungry. And if Jesse hadn't lit that moss...

He pictured the moment again — the flare, the toss, the hesitation in those big dark eyes before the retreat. Fire still mattered out here. It wasn't just destruction. It was protection. He sat there for a while longer, his body slowly remembering that it could rest. That it was allowed to. But part of his mind stayed awake now. The part that had moved faster than thought when something with teeth came looking.

The part that understood this: nothing was going to save him out here. If he made it out alive, it would be because he earned it.

He didn't lie down again. He couldn't. Every time he shifted his weight or closed his eyes, he imagined the bear's shape sliding between the trees again, quiet as steam off hot stone. So he sat through the night, leaning against the upturned roots, arms around his knees, the Pulaski balanced across his lap like a blade from some old-world sentinel.

By the time the horizon bled faint light, Jesse's eyes burned with fatigue, but his mind was alert, grounded, focused in a way it hadn't been in days. He packed quickly. The tarp folded unevenly, stiff with ash and soot. His canteen felt lighter than he remembered — another problem for another hour. The Pulaski swung onto his shoulder like it belonged there, like it had earned its place.

Jesse paused once before leaving camp and looked toward the path the bear had taken. Nothing moved.

"Thanks for the lesson," he said softly.

It wasn't sarcasm. It wasn't a joke. He meant it. Then he turned his back on the trees and started walking east, following no trail but his own.

Chapter 15

Jesse first saw the tape around midmorning, though it was hard to tell what time it really was anymore. Every direction looked like a waiting room between dusk and something worse. He was moving slowly, not because of fatigue — although that was still there, curled tight around the base of his spine like a weight — but because the air had changed again. Still dry, still ash-choked, but calmer somehow. Less hostile.

The tape looked like bark at first. A torn shred of orange dangling from a high branch. He might have passed it by if it hadn't fluttered once, catching the wind at just the right moment. Something about the color made him stop.

He moved closer, heart picking up as he reached for it. The end of the ribbon was brittle, curled from heat. It tore in his fingers as he pulled it down, but the loop remained on the branch, tied with a practiced hand — loop, twist, tug. Standard flagging knot. Fire crew. Black letters bled across the orange like a ghost still trying to be heard.

"Dozer line start →"

He blinked. Then blinked again, just to make sure he wasn't seeing it wrong. He hadn't seen flagging since the controlled burn days ago — not since everything went to hell. Not since the fire had jumped and the smoke had swallowed the sky. He turned slowly in the direction the arrow pointed, squinting past the trees. Twenty, maybe thirty yards ahead — another flag. Then another. A trail.

"Someone was here," Jesse said, not even trying to keep the disbelief out of his voice.

He followed the next flag, then the next. Each was worn, stiff with soot, and tied to low branches or nailed into trunks. The spacing was irregular, but the direction was clear — someone had been cutting a line here. Years ago, maybe longer, but it was real. Crews had passed through this place. Men and women with tools and helmets, sweating under smoke, arguing over chainsaw fuel and line depth. People like him. Or like he used to be, before this all changed. It didn't matter that the ground had shifted since then, that storms had pulled flags loose or dropped trees over old marks. The history was still here. The bones of the line.

As he walked, he began to see more signs — red and pink ribbons mixed in with the orange, denoting different phases or crews. Some were wrapped around trunks. Others were tacked beside spray-painted arrows pointing across slopes and gullies. The brush had grown back in some places, obscuring the old trail, but he pushed through. He wasn't just following tape now. He was walking in footsteps. A laminated card hung from a nail, cracked and nearly opaque. He peeled it open just enough to read the faint lettering:

Weather Log – B Shift – Day 3.

No date. No crew number. But it made his throat tighten. He reached a place where the brush cleared out naturally — a shallow ridge hollowed by wind and runoff. There, the signs grew thicker. Two broken shovels lay half-buried in the duff, their blades flaking with rust. A bundle of old hose had collapsed in on itself like a sleeping snake, its canvas sides eaten through by mold. He crouched beside it and ran his fingers across the weave.

"How long ago?" he murmured. "How long before the forest decided to take you back?"

He moved on, walking carefully now, like the trail deserved respect. Up ahead, a long gash in the dirt angled across a slope. A firebreak — barely visible, but still etched into the land like scar tissue. Jesse followed it with his eyes and saw a tree, thick and blackened, still standing despite the burn. The bark had split wide from heat and age. At eye level, someone had carved into it. Letters. Rough, shallow, but deliberate.

"TB + JB / Crew 6"

Jesse stared at the initials. The second one stopped him cold.

JB.

His fingers brushed the carving, not touching the letters directly but tracing their edges, as if doing so would reveal the name in full. His father's initials had been JB. Jesse Brooks. Just like his. He stood there, unmoving, and the world around him faded to a blur. The wind stirred the ash in the trees. A single ribbon behind him fluttered once and went still.

He didn't speak. Didn't need to. The forest didn't say anything back. But in the silence, something shifted in him. Like a hand had pressed against his chest and reminded his heart to beat stronger. Not faster. Just clearer. He wasn't just out here trying not to die anymore. He was going to make it out. Because someone had carved their name into this place and left a path. And he had found it.

He didn't move for a long time. He stayed by the tree with the carved initials, fingertips hovering just above the bark, breathing slow and shallow like anything louder might erase the moment. There was no way to know if it was really his dad. JB could've meant a dozen names. Maybe a hundred, if you counted every rookie who ever scrawled initials on a fire line.

But in that second, Jesse didn't doubt. His father had walked here. On this slope. Through this brush. Carrying the same weight he carried now. Same heat. Same fear. Same silence. They had stood in the same air, maybe decades apart, and both of them had left marks.

He took a step back and looked around the clearing. There were no birds here, no squirrel chatter, no deer trails etched into the ash. Just remnants. Hose. Flagging tape. Burned metal. Time worn down to essentials. The perfect place for ghosts to live.

He didn't want to walk away without saying something. Not out loud — he wasn't ready for that —

but something visible. Something physical. Something that would last longer than a whisper.

He moved slowly toward a flat spot by the base of the carved tree and crouched. The soil here was dark, untouched by recent flame. It felt like the ground had been holding this memory in its palm, waiting for someone to come back and notice.

He began gathering stones. Some were still warm from the sun, others slick with ash, but he wiped them clean and stacked them carefully. One at a time. A circle at the base. Then a tighter second layer. Then a few more to seal the top. It wasn't tall — barely a foot — but it stood clean and centered. A cairn.

He reached into his pack and pulled out a small section of charcoal — one of the stubs he hadn't used yet. He turned it over in his fingers, then knelt beside the stone pile and carefully wrote **"JB"** on the face of the largest, flattest rock near the top.

It wasn't for identification. It was for connection. For permission to keep going. When he was done, he rested his fingers on the stone.

"Thanks," Jesse said quietly. "For being here first."

He stood, brushed the dirt from his palms, and tightened the shoulder straps on his pack.

He didn't feel fixed. But something had realigned. Some wire inside him that had gone slack over the last few days was pulling taut again. Not to the point of snapping. Just enough to hold him upright.

He looked east, then down toward a shallow fold in the land. The fire wasn't gone. The smoke still curled low behind the trees. But the weight of it had shifted. Now it was just another thing between him and where he needed to be. He stepped over the fireline trench and left the clearing, the initials, and the cairn standing quiet like a memory made solid.

Chapter 16

Jesse was mid-climb when he heard it. A distant thrum, almost too low to register at first — like something buried beneath the wind, steady and pulsing. He paused, frowning, one hand braced against a sun-bleached boulder, but the sound slipped away again, lost in the hush of heat and altitude.

The climb was brutal. Not the steepest slope he'd faced, but the longest — a relentless, grinding ascent along a jagged ridgeline littered with scorched pine needles and loose, splintered rock. His calves burned. His shoulders screamed beneath the pack. The Pulaski dragged against his spine with every step, heavy and deliberate, as if reminding him: *You chose this.*

The trees thinned the higher he climbed, not burned this time but starved by elevation. Shrubs gave way to exposed stone. The shade disappeared. The air felt brittle now — thin and metallic, like breathing through gauze. Even the insects had fallen behind.

Then he heard it again. Stronger. Closer. A rhythmic chopping, hidden behind the wind. Not natural. Something mechanical, but not yet clear. He kept moving, the incline forcing him to crawl at times, fingers digging into gravel that broke beneath his hands. The sound rose and fell like breath — drawing closer, then slipping behind ridgelines again. He scrambled up the slope, knees shaking, lungs scraping for oxygen.

At the final stretch, his boots slipped on a patch of shale. He caught himself on a root, chest heaving, ears straining toward the rhythm echoing now through the upper air. He pushed the last twenty feet with teeth clenched, the summit cresting in front of him like the edge of a world.

And then he was there — standing on the ridgeline, chest to the wind, eyes sweeping the open sky. The sound snapped into focus. Out across the valley — five miles off, maybe less — something moved. Small. Fast.

Darting between folds of the land like a dragonfly skating the wind. A helicopter.

Jesse froze. His heart leaped into his throat, almost painful in how fast it slammed against his ribs. He squinted hard, wiping sweat from his brow with a trembling hand. Yes. A chopper. Light-colored. Civilian, maybe. Or forestry. Flying low. Slow. Surveying.

"Hey!" he shouted, his voice cracking.

He waved one arm over his head, then both. Jumped twice. "Over here!"

Nothing.

The helicopter kept moving, banking westward, the angle shifting. No signal from the cockpit. No change in altitude. Jesse yanked off his pack, digging fast, hands scrambling for the silver emergency blanket. He stood and snapped it open, letting the light hit the reflective surface. He angled it toward the sun, catching and bouncing what little light he could into the open air.

The chopper didn't turn. Didn't pause. Didn't drop height. It slid sideways behind a ridge and vanished.

"Damn it!" he shouted, his voice raw now.

He dropped the blanket. It fell over his boots like an accusation. He stood there for several long seconds, breathing hard, fists clenched, trying to hold together the sudden, brutal burst of adrenaline and disappointment that came from seeing rescue and watching it slip away.

Then he turned slowly and looked back the way he'd come. The smoke was thicker in that direction. Down below, maybe a mile or two, the fire was still moving. That dangerous kind of low fire that crawled under leaf litter and came alive again when the wind shifted.

"I need cover," he muttered.

No one answered.

But the slope to his right had potential. A shallow bench beneath a rock ledge. Enough loose dirt for a trench. Not great. But something. He reached for his pack, rolled his shoulders, and pulled the Pulaski free. Then he started digging.

It wasn't clean work, but he didn't stop.

Three inches deep. Then six. Then ten. It just had to be ready. The sun, filtered through haze, gave him no sense of time. But sweat poured from him like a leaking hose. His arms burned. His legs shook. He didn't care.

"Just like last time," Jesse muttered, gritting his teeth as he pried out another root ball.

By the time he stopped, the trench was roughly six feet long, maybe two feet wide, and a little over a foot and a half deep. Enough to lie flat. He lined the bottom with debris — old pine boughs, scraped dirt, and flattened his emergency blanket to keep the soil off his back. Then he pulled whatever loose material he could gather for a cover. His tarp stretched tight between two fallen limbs. A jacket. Dead ferns.

He sat at the edge, panting, covered in ash and soil, the Pulaski blade resting on his knee. He didn't look heroic. He didn't feel ready. But the trench was done. And if the fire came tonight, he had a fighting chance.

He took a slow drink from his canteen, then checked the sky. Smoke still drifted. The wind was inconsistent — soft now, then gusting. He could smell char in the air, feel the subtle shift of heat in the trees. No visible flame yet. But soon.

He wiped his face with a filthy sleeve, then lay back into the trench for the first time, testing the fit. His shoulders touched both sides. His knees bent slightly. He let his hands fall across his chest. The earth was warm beneath him. It didn't feel like a threat now. It felt like armor. But it wasn't comfortable either. It pressed against his hips and shoulders, dirt clinging to his skin, pine needles poking through the blanket he'd laid down. The tarp above him sagged slightly where he hadn't tensioned it properly. But it didn't matter. He didn't need comfort. He needed something he could hold.

He lay flat, staring up through the half-canopy, watching the sky go from dirty orange to slate gray. The smoke thickened and thinned with the breeze, never fully leaving. Somewhere below, the fire was still creeping. He could feel it more than hear it — a pressure on the back of the wind, a warmth that hadn't been there an hour ago.

He turned his head and scanned the ridge. From here, he could see a long arc of trees, most of them dead or fire-scarred, standing like blackened spears. The land dropped away steeply to the south, where the fireline had once held — now breached, now forgotten. He tried the radio again, not expecting anything.

"Jesse Brooks, Bravo Crew. I'm on the high ridge east of Sector 9. I saw a helicopter this morning, no response. I've dug in. Fire's behind me. Still moving. Still alive."

He waited. Static. Then nothing. He clipped it back onto his chest. There was a time, maybe three days ago, when that silence would've unraveled him. The lack of contact. The stillness. The isolation. He would've raged or panicked or whispered someone's name just to break the air. But now? Now he just listened. Let it be quiet.

Let the wind speak when it wanted to. He closed his eyes for a moment and breathed deeply. Not to sleep. Just to remember that his lungs still worked and that the fire hadn't taken them yet.

Chapter 17

The glow on the horizon had deepened from a soft flicker to a pulsing amber wall. It rose between the trees like sunrise at the wrong angle — low, orange, and hungry. It wasn't loud yet, but Jesse knew better than to trust that. The quiet ones were worse. The slow, crawling fire that hugged the ground, licked at roots, built in silence before flashing up the moment wind gave it permission.

He sat up in the trench, feeling the air shift. The breeze now came from behind him, down the slope, toward the fire. That meant the fire would follow. It would crawl uphill, pulled by heat and terrain, just like the training slides had shown. And he was right in its path.

He didn't panic. But he didn't waste time, either. He rolled over and opened the outside flap of his pack, fingers working quickly despite how numb they felt. The shelter was still there — folded in tight silver layers, heat-crinkled at the edges but intact. He'd checked it every day. Every night. Not because he wanted to use it, but because not checking it would've been worse, like inviting fate to find a weak spot. He didn't use it during the lighting fire. He didn't need to. But this fire? This fire was no joke.

Now there were no more excuses. He unrolled it carefully, checking seams, opening the breathing flap, and threading the foot anchors through loops with shaking hands. Then he laid it beside the trench and stared at it. This thing had always felt more like a body bag than protection. He'd seen the videos. Read the after-action reports. Shelters worked — sometimes. When terrain, luck, and timing all lined up, the outcome was favorable. But they weren't built for guarantees. They were built for last chances.

"You wait too long," he murmured, "and you die inside it."

The wind picked up again, warmer this time. The scent of pine turned bitter. Smoke began to creep between the trees, low to the ground like fog that had learned to crawl. He took one long drink from his canteen, wiped his mouth, and sealed it tight. Then he rolled the shelter open fully, pulled it over his body, and slid into the trench.

The world narrowed fast — silver on all sides, dirt below, his breath bouncing off heat-reflective walls. He settled flat, face turned to the opening flap. The sound outside dimmed to a muffled hush, like being wrapped in foil and buried alive. He pulled the edges tight and anchored the corners with loose rock and his own body weight.

"Stay down," he told himself.

His cheek pressed to the dirt, the air already warming around him. He let out a sharp breath and whispered, "Why do I keep going back to green fuel?"

It wasn't the first time he'd wondered. Burned ground was safer. Burned ground didn't reignite. But green meant something else. Water. Shelter. The chance of food. You didn't find ponds in the black. You didn't find tree cover or shade or even direction. Fire left everything behind scorched and flat and useless. You followed the burn long enough, you stopped being a survivor and started being a ghost. That's what no one told you in training.

"I go back," he said softly, "because the black doesn't care if I make it. But the green might."

He swallowed, eyes closed tight. "I just have to survive it."

The smoke pressed harder. Then, beyond the fabric, he heard it: the whispering edge of the fire. The sound came first, like wind, but thicker. Like air being torn apart. Then came the heat. He felt it building before the flames ever reached him. Not touching yet, but arriving — radiating from the slope like a fever crawling over the land. The emergency shelter crinkled around him, and the seams near his ears began to pop. The temperature inside jumped with every breath, sweat pooling beneath his clothes, his skin slick, lips already cracking. He pressed his face down toward the dirt and tried to breathe shallowly.

Smoke found its way in anyway. He could taste pine resin and ash and the burn of something synthetic carried in the heat. His hands clenched instinctively against the sides of the shelter. The silver film felt like the inside of a pan left on a hot stove.

He whispered, "Stay down," but the words stuck in his throat.

Time stopped behaving. One second stretched into forever. Then everything blurred. The sound outside changed — louder, closer — like the fire had reached the trees above the trench. The wind screamed past the fabric. Ash and debris pattered against the top like a hundred tiny fists. His breath came faster. His ribs ached. His pulse thudded in his skull like a second heart. He felt his thoughts begin to slide. Not away from consciousness exactly, but away from *here*. Like his body had agreed to hold on, but his mind refused to stay in the trench. It took him somewhere else. Somewhere safer. Somewhere older.

He was ten, crouched beside the fire pit in the backyard, knees buried in the brittle grass, watching his dad twist newspaper into tight little knots for kindling. The sun had just gone down, leaving the sky streaked in violet and rust, and the air held that crisp bite of late October — sharp enough to sting the nose but not enough to drive them inside. Leaves rustled across the patio in slow, dry drifts. They'd raked earlier, Jesse and his dad, piling gold and brown into mounds that never stayed put.

His fingers had been stained with dirt. His dad's hands were black at the knuckles from chimney soot. They'd laughed about something — Jesse didn't remember what — and the echo of it still rang faintly in the memory.

The scent of woodsmoke started before the match even touched the kindling, like it lived in the pit itself. It was the kind of smoke that clung to jackets, the kind that made his mom wrinkle her nose and wave them toward the laundry room whenever they came back inside.

His dad leaned over the fire pit, match in one hand, one knee down, the other elbow balanced on his thigh. The flame flared, wavered, then licked forward, catching the newspaper first, then the dry sticks arranged in a careful pyramid. Light danced on the bricks. The fire made a soft popping sound as it found its voice.

"You know why it works?" his dad asked, squinting at the flicker. His voice was calm, the kind that meant a lesson was coming.

Jesse shook his head. He didn't speak. Just watched.

His dad gave that half-smile — the one he reserved for these moments, when something mattered but didn't need to be heavy.

"Because it wants to," his dad said. "Fire wants to burn. That's all it knows. All it's ever known."

The words settled into Jesse's chest. He didn't fully understand them then, but he remembered how they sounded. How sure they were.

His dad reached forward, gently nudging one of the sticks with a poker, coaxing the flame higher. The firelight caught his face — orange along the jaw, deep shadows in his eyes. He looked older in that light. Not tired, just serious. A keeper of knowledge.

"Our job," he said, leaning a little closer, "is to make sure it doesn't forget who's in charge."

Then he tapped Jesse on the chest with two fingers. "And that starts here."

Jesse had looked down at his own chest like the words might leave a mark. Maybe they had. The memory evaporated as Jesse coughed. The heat was worse now. Inside the shelter, the air was thick. His vision swam. He pressed his cheek to the dirt and opened the air flap just enough to sip what little oxygen drifted in. The world narrowed again. His heartbeat slowed, then surged. He was floating. He was nowhere. He was still here. Then everything went dark.

Chapter 18

The first thing Jesse noticed was the silence. It pressed against his ears, heavy and unnatural, as if the fire had scorched away sound itself. He lay motionless in the trench for what felt like a long time, too disoriented to sit up, too sore to draw a full breath. His ribs throbbed in dull waves. His throat felt raw, stripped down to the lining. Each blink pulled grit across his eyes like sandpaper. The smoke still hung low in the air — not thick, but persistent, as though the forest hadn't yet decided to let him breathe freely. Every inhale carried the taste of char, the sharp edge of carbon and ash that stung the corners of his mouth and coated his tongue in bitterness.

He coughed once and instantly regretted it. His lungs seized, cramping as hot air clawed its way back out. The motion sent a jolt through his chest, and he rolled to one side, bracing himself on an elbow that barely held his weight. The emergency shelter lay crumpled across his legs, the silver skin buckled and blackened at the edges, curling like burnt paper. It looked like a thing that had been swallowed whole and spit back up. He peeled it away slowly, wincing at the sting where the fabric had clung to skin too long exposed to heat. His forearms were tender. His calves felt sunburned from the inside out.

The memory of what had just happened came in fragments — the press of smoke, the heat crawling over the dirt, the sound of ash pelting the tarp like sleet. He didn't remember the moment he blacked out, only the build-up: the pressure behind his eyes, the whispering roar growing louder, the way everything tightened in on itself until the world vanished behind his eyelids. He didn't feel like he'd slept. He felt like he'd gone somewhere else and barely come back.

When he stood, it was slow and uneven, his legs uncertain beneath him. One knee popped, and the other nearly buckled. The trench had partially collapsed on the far side, the scorched earth marking a crude oval where fire had passed around and over him. The perimeter told a clear story — flame had licked the edge of the hollow, curled around the trench like it had considered him, then moved on.

He took a few steps, testing his balance, feeling the fatigue settle deep into his bones. The ridge around him had transformed. Trees stood without leaves, their limbs burned away, leaving only upright husks of barkless trunks. The underbrush had vanished completely. What little green had existed before the fire was gone now, erased as if it had never been. The ground crunched under his boots, a brittle surface of ash and scorched stone interrupted only by small craters where embers had punched into the soil.

Off to his right, a faint sound stirred — something shifting just beyond a wisp of smoke. He turned toward it, eyes narrowing, every nerve still wound tight from the fire. Through the haze, a shape emerged. Human. Upright. Watching. Too far to make out clearly, but undeniably there. His heart slammed hard once, and he opened his mouth to speak, but no sound came. His voice cracked, and his lips felt welded shut by soot. When he wiped at his eyes and looked again, the shape was gone. Vanished like it had never been there.

He stared at the space it had occupied, willing it to return, but the smoke moved without answers. Only the soft hiss of settling debris met his ears, and the faint whisper of wind threading through skeletal branches. He turned back toward the trench to ground himself, but something about the slope had changed. The geography of the ridge didn't look the same. It twisted in ways he didn't recognize. Even the angles felt wrong, the grade slightly off from where he thought he'd crawled up. He blinked again, but the disorientation didn't fade.

Another figure appeared, farther this time, near a cluster of rocks half-buried in ash. This one hunched slightly, holding something. It could've been Riley. The posture was familiar. Jesse squinted through the blur of heat and smoke, trying to lock in details, but before he could focus, the figure shifted and dissolved like steam breaking apart in wind.

His breath came faster, and he gripped the Pulaski hard enough to ache. These weren't theatrical hallucinations with wild colors and impossible logic. They were too real. Too mundane. Just people — or things that looked like people — appearing in silence, watching him, then vanishing as if they'd simply stepped out of existence. That quiet normalcy made them worse.

He dropped to a crouch beside the trench, fingers pressed to his knees to steady his breath.

"You're still coming down from the fire," he muttered aloud, voice dry and cracked. "Low oxygen. Stress. You're seeing things."

But he didn't believe it. Not really. The next shape to rise through the haze was a child. Small frame. Bare feet. Standing perfectly still in a patch of earth burned so clean it looked sterile. The boy lifted one arm and pointed — down the slope, toward the valley. The direction Jesse had already been heading. The message, if it was one, didn't feel ominous. It felt... resigned. Then the boy faded from view like dust rising on heat.

He didn't speak after that. There was nothing left to say. He stood, brushed ash from his jeans in long downward strokes, and adjusted the pack on his shoulders. The Pulaski moved with him, balanced now. He set one foot forward and began walking again.

The slope was sharp, the footing treacherous. Beneath the layer of ash, slick patches of exposed clay waited to slide. In some places, the trail narrowed to little more than rock shelves held together by roots that had already died. He moved slowly at first, testing each step, but momentum crept in. Whether from gravity or something else, his pace increased.

He didn't consciously try to move faster. But he felt watched. The hallucinations hadn't vanished. They had simply evolved. Now it was motion he caught at the corners of his vision. A flicker behind a tree. A shoulder disappearing behind a trunk. The breeze carried no leaves, yet sometimes he heard footsteps parallel to his own, pacing him.

The pain in his body pulsed with every step. His legs ached. His left knee flared with sharp warnings whenever the incline steepened. His lungs still rasped from the shelter, his breath shallow. And behind his eyes, a steady throb pulsed like a fault line waiting to crack. But none of it stopped him. The rhythm of movement held him together.

At one point, he passed what looked like Ortiz — seated on a fallen log, carving a stick with quiet focus. Jesse didn't break stride. He didn't glance again. A few minutes later, light spilled suddenly through a break in the canopy, just one golden shaft angled like a spotlight through dust. The ash glowed where the sunlight touched it. He stood in it for a beat, let it warm his cheeks, then moved on. The forest closed over the light like a curtain falling.

Time slid sideways. Minutes and hours blended. Hunger no longer felt urgent. He'd eaten his last bar the day before the firestorm, biting it in the dark without tasting. Now, the emptiness in his gut felt clinical — less like a need, more like a fact.

Then he saw his father — not a memory this time, but as he'd looked the day of the funeral. The image stood between two trees, arms crossed, head slightly tilted. Jesse didn't stop.

"I know," he whispered, and walked past.

Eventually, the trees began to thin. The slope leveled under his feet, and ash gave way to churned soil. Jesse moved with automatic steps, attention dulled by dehydration and smoke exposure, until the ground shifted beneath him. The trees had been blasted outward here in a strange, circular pattern, the fire's signature left behind like the impact of a bomb.

He paused at the edge of the clearing and took it in. What lay before him wasn't just another stretch of burned forest. This had been a campsite. He could see it in the blackened bones of the scene — the sag of collapsed frames, the scorched outlines of gear that had once been essential. The plastic from a food bin had melted into the dirt like spilled tar. A sleeping bag, or what remained of one, had fused with the rocks. A section of tarp had curled and hardened into a grotesque spiral.

His breath caught as his eyes landed on something half-buried near the edge of it all. A hand. Or what was left of one. Curled inward like it had reached for something in the end — for protection, for air, for help. The skin was charred and cracked, bone showing through in one place. There were no clothes, no other parts visible. Just the hand, clenched and blackened, waiting in silence.

He couldn't move for a moment. His pulse thudded in his ears. That wasn't debris. That wasn't a hallucination. That was someone. A person who had been here, probably sleeping or laughing or sipping from a water bottle, never knowing that a wildfire had been nearby. Never knowing it was coming until it was already too late.

The worst part about it, Jesse knew where the fire had started. He knew how far it had jumped. He remembered the training op, the drip torches, the alarms in Basecamp, the missing weather shift that had turned everything on its head. This blaze hadn't started naturally. It had started under a plan. A plan his crew had been part of. A plan he had stood inside. Maybe it wasn't his match that lit the ridge, but it didn't matter.

"I should've found them," he murmured, voice hoarse and raw. "I should've—"

He didn't finish. What would he have done? Warned them? Carried them out? He'd barely made it himself. Still, the guilt stuck, because no one had found them. No helicopter had lifted them out. No crew had flagged their location. No one had marked their passing — not until now, not until him. Jesse, who stumbled into the aftermath days too late, smelling of smoke, dragging a half-melted pack and a half-dead body.

He looked back at the hand. Part of him wanted to dig, to uncover the rest of whoever had been there, to know their name. But another part whispered that it was better not to see. Better to let them rest in the scorched earth they had died in. Instead, he bowed his head for a long moment. It wasn't prayer, exactly. It was apology.

In the center of the ruined camp, where a fire ring had once held warmth and light, he spotted something. A knife. The handle poked from the ash, angled cleanly as if it had been placed rather than dropped. He stepped toward it slowly, boots crunching through the brittle remains of tarp and cloth. He crouched beside the fire ring and reached for the knife, brushing away the powdery soot with one hand.

The sheath was partly melted, but the blade inside slid free without resistance, untouched by the fire that had eaten everything else. He turned it in his hand, feeling the weight. The grip molded to his fingers like it belonged there. It wasn't just a tool. It was a tether — to whoever had owned it, to whatever survival they'd tried for, to the last stand they hadn't won. He slid the sheath onto his belt, adjusted it for comfort, and stood again.

He didn't leave right away. He walked the perimeter of the camp, slow and steady, trying to read the story written in the ruins. A campsite like this didn't vanish overnight. Someone had planned to be here. Maybe for days. Maybe for longer. But fire didn't care about plans. It only needed wind and fuel and time. And he had walked through plenty of fuel. He'd seen how fast it moved. How quiet. How lethal.

He took a breath and looked toward the far side of the clearing. The slope continued downhill, still marked by soot and ruin, but beyond it, the trees looked spaced farther apart. The smoke had begun to lift in patches, and the light had a cooler tone. The worst of the fire was behind him. But the consequences were not.

He gave one last look to the camp — to the broken outlines, the ghosted gear, and the single burned hand — then turned and continued walking.

Chapter 19

Jesse's footsteps crunched dully over the cinder-laced soil, but it felt distant, like hearing himself from underwater. His legs carried him forward on autopilot. The knife hung at his belt, bouncing gently with each step. It gave him a strange kind of comfort, the way a compass might, or the memory of someone steady walking beside you. He hadn't seen another hallucination in hours. He wasn't sure if that meant he was getting better or worse.

The land had begun to flatten, which helped. The slope had given way to rolling terrain, scattered with old stumps and the skeletons of what had once been a young forest. He paused to drink from a shallow puddle that had collected in a rock basin — rain from days ago, maybe, or water condensed from ash-laden fog. It tasted like char, but it was wet. He filled the cap twice, sipped it down, then moved on.

The ashfall thickened again. Within minutes, it coated his boots so completely he could barely see the tread. He stopped wiping his face. It was a losing battle. His eyes burned. His lips had split in three places. But there was still something keeping him upright — not adrenaline anymore, something quieter. The stubborn will that had carried him through the shelter, through the hallucinations, through the moment when he could've sat down and stopped and hadn't. And then, through the haze, he saw it.

Structure.

It was barely visible — a jagged silhouette against the pale, ash-choked horizon. Rectangular, a roof still mostly intact. Not large enough to be a ranger station, but too deliberate to be a natural formation. His heart didn't leap. There wasn't enough energy left for hope to burn hot anymore. But it tightened, as if some part of him deeper than thought had been watching for this all along.

He picked up his pace. The building grew clearer with every step, its black frame emerging like a memory unburied. As he got closer, he saw that it had been a single-room structure once — a cabin or outpost, possibly fire crew-built, maybe temporary. The siding had been mostly consumed by flame. Two walls remained standing. The others had collapsed inward, half-burying whatever was inside.

He stepped carefully around the front, finding the edge of what had once been a doorframe. The hinges still held part of the door, though it was warped and split. He pushed it open with the toe of his boot and leaned in. The air inside smelled worse than outside. Not fresh smoke — old. Cooked. Burned plastic and metal, and beneath that, something faintly sour. He stood at the threshold, eyes scanning the blackened interior before stepping inside.

The floor was mostly gone. Where planks had once covered the ground, there was now a thin crust of charred beams and sagging boards that cracked softly beneath his boots. He stepped lightly, scanning the inside of the small structure — it couldn't have been more than twelve feet wide, the walls bowed inward, the roof sagging in one corner like a shoulder that had finally given out.

The smell was stronger here. Not just fire. Something else. Old rot or cooked flesh, he couldn't tell. He kept breathing shallow through his nose, trying not to imagine it. The light filtering through the smoke outside wasn't enough to fully illuminate the space, so he crouched and angled his head, letting his eyes adjust.

There were signs of habitation — not recent, but not ancient either. A metal cot frame leaned against the far wall, twisted and blackened, the mattress long incinerated. A scorched backpack lay half under it, half melted into the floor. He reached for it cautiously, brushing ash away with the edge of his glove. The zipper was fused shut, but one side had already split. Inside, he found something wrapped in foil and plastic — a food bar, nearly intact. He broke off a corner and sniffed it.

It smelled like smoke and peanut butter. He ate it anyway. The chew was dry and chalky. He didn't care. It filled his mouth with paste and grit, and he swallowed it down with effort, chasing it with a sip of his last inch of water. He knew it wouldn't hold long, but it was something. It was fuel.

He stood again, wiping his lips, and turned toward what had drawn his eye from the door — a shape near the rear corner of the shelter, beneath the beam collapse.

A blanket. Covered in a layer of fine ash, like everything else, it looked like a drift — a pile of forgotten laundry. Jesse approached slowly, pulse rising without reason. He didn't want to uncover it. He already knew what was beneath.

There was no point. Whoever this had been — they'd come here for shelter, same as him. Maybe they'd thought they could wait it out. Maybe they'd been trapped. Maybe they'd chosen not to run anymore. He didn't judge them. He didn't feel sorry for them, either. He just silently blamed himself again. What he felt, standing there in that cinder-laced ruin, was something colder. Recognition. This had almost been *him*.

He reached down beside the sleeping bag, careful not to disturb the remains, and pulled out a dented metal can — beans, label mostly gone but lid intact. He slipped it into his pack. Then he saw something beneath the collapsed beam — a handle.

The second knife. It was buried up to the hilt, partially melted into the wood, but he worked it free. The blade was curved, dull from heat, but still solid. Smaller than the one on his hip. He ran his thumb along the spine and nodded.

"You lasted longer than most," he said, voice hoarse.

He stood and looked around the shelter one last time. No more gear, maps, or notes. Nothing else useful. Just ashes, bones, and whatever memories the forest hadn't already reclaimed.

He stepped outside, brushing soot from his chest, and pulled the door shut behind him. He stood in the ashfall a long moment, holding the new knife in one hand, letting the world settle again. Then he walked away, leaving the memories he would never speak of behind.

The slope beside the structure wasn't high, just enough of a rise to give him elevation above the smoke-choked clearing. He climbed it slowly, boots slipping in loose cinders, his thighs screaming with each step. The sky overhead had gone pale again, a colorless dome with no shape to it. The air had cooled slightly, or maybe he had just gone numb. Either way, he didn't trust it.

When he reached the top of the knoll, he stood still for a long moment, hands on his hips, breathing heavily. He felt older. Every movement carried weight now, like gravity itself had thickened since the fire. His skin still stung from the shelter burn, his lips were bleeding, and his shirt hung damp and black with soot. But none of it mattered. What mattered was what he could see.

The valley stretched below him, wide and gray, framed by hills that had burned unevenly. Some slopes were stripped bare, others still held stands of blackened trees. Smoke still coiled in slow drifts, but it wasn't rising anymore. The fire had moved on, leaving only its shadow behind.

He turned slowly, squinting against the haze. At first, it all looked the same — ash, ruin, more trees. But then his eyes locked on a narrow line running across a ridge in the distance. It didn't match the terrain. It was too straight and cleen.

"Is that a road?" he whispered, more to himself than anything else. The forest out here didn't care enough to answer him.

It could've been gravel. Maybe a fire access. But it was something manmade. Something that led somewhere. He stared at it, trying not to blink too long in case it disappeared like everything else lately had. But it held. And below it, just barely visible through the smoke: a tower. Maybe a repeater, a lookout —or maybe salvation.

He crouched in the dirt, feeling it crumble under his boots, and pulled out the can of food from the cabin. He stabbed it open with the smaller knife, peeled back the lid, and ate what was inside, cold, metallic, and unidentifiable. He didn't taste it, really. Just used it to help him keep going. When the can was empty, he set it aside, wiped his face with the cleanest corner of his sleeve, and stood again. The wind shifted. This time it didn't carry smoke — only silence. And in that silence, Jesse spoke out loud. "I'm going to make it."

Chapter 20

The rocks beneath Jesse's boots had been loose for miles — scorched, softened by heat, then cooled into glassy shards that cracked like eggshells under weight. He should've slowed his descent. But the sight of the tower had lit something dangerous inside him — urgency. That's what did it. Hope. He stepped onto a flat stone, felt it shift, and instinctively threw his weight forward to catch himself. His foot dropped fast — faster than it should've — and landed square on something hard and jagged: a piece of rebar embedded in a burned-out stump.

Pain exploded up his leg. Not sharp at first. A dry, brutal snap followed by heat. He yelped — a strange, raw sound — and toppled sideways, sliding a short distance before slamming into a split log that caught him hard in the ribs. He lay there for several seconds, blinking at the smoke-colored sky, stunned by how fast everything had changed.

His foot throbbed. He reached down slowly, gritting his teeth, and pulled his leg closer to inspect it. The boot was already black with ash and caked mud — but now a darker wetness bloomed around the arch. When he touched it, pain roared up his spine like an electric current. He groaned, tugged the boot off with shaking hands, and peeled the sock back.

Blood.

A jagged tear ran diagonally across the bottom of his foot, just below the ball. Clean, deep, and ugly. It was already swelling.

"God," he muttered. "You idiot."

He set the boot down beside him, and that's when he noticed it — the sole was damaged. Worn past the tread. The rubber had thinned and bubbled like tar in spots, melted and reformed in rough ridges. He turned it slightly. The section beneath the arch had split, the foam inside brittle and crumbling like charcoal. No support left. No protection. The heat over the past few days had ruined the integrity, and he hadn't noticed until now.

He felt his stomach twist. A broken boot wasn't supposed to be what took him out. But maybe that's how it always happened — a thousand little problems wearing you down until one of them hit the wrong way.

He looked around the slope for shelter, something flat or dry, but there was nothing but charred debris and scorched dirt. Just cinders and blackened wood. He picked the least hostile log and dragged himself over, pulling out his kit as he went. The gauze roll was dirty, having been opened and closed a dozen times. He used it anyway, pressing a folded section into the wound and hissing through his teeth as fresh pressure set his nerves on fire.

It wasn't enough. The bleeding kept coming — slower now, but steady. He closed his eyes, reached for the knife at his belt, and made the decision in one breath.

"You're going to sew it," he told himself. "That's what you're going to do."

It wasn't a question, it was a demand. He didn't have a real needle. Just a bent safety pin, rusty at the hinge, but narrow enough. He pried it from the flap of his pack, wiped it on the inside of his shirt, then held it over the lighter flame until it glowed faintly red. Not sterilized, but close enough.

Next, a lace from his boot. He cut it clean with the smaller knife and unraveled the threads until he had one long, fraying line. It wasn't perfect. It didn't need to be. It just needed to get the job done.

His fingers trembled. His mouth was dry. Ash clung to the sweat on his forearms. He tied a strip of cloth above the wound as a makeshift tourniquet and braced his foot against the log. He took a deep breath, exhaled once. Then he drove the pin through.

Pain lit up his whole body. He didn't scream, not fully, but the sound that came out of him was animal. Jaw locked. Eyes wide. He forced the point through the other side of the wound and pulled the thread behind it. Again. Then again. Each stitch a new firework of agony behind his eyes. Each tug made his foot twitch and cramp, but he didn't stop. He kept going. Knotting the thread. Tightening the torn skin until the gash began to close in jagged peaks.

By the time he tied off the last stitch, the world had gone slightly sideways. He slumped against the log. His hands shook and sweat soaked his collar. But the bleeding had stopped. The wound wasn't pretty, but it held. When the spinning slowed, he pulled out a strip of old shirt from his side pouch — sun-bleached, wrinkled, but dry — and wrapped it tightly around the sutures.

He just sat, arms draped over his knees, letting the ache pulse through him in steady waves. He looked up at the sky. It was still gray with smoke, but he could see shape behind it now. The outline of clouds where the horizon used to be. He clenched his jaw, reached for the branch he'd been using as a walking stick, and braced himself.

"Back on it," he said, voice a gravel whisper.

He stood slowly, dragging his injured foot beneath him, testing weight, adjusting. It barely held, but it held. He didn't think about the miles left. Or the road. Or whether the tower had ever been real. He didn't think about what came next. He only thought about the next step.

"One more day," he whispered. "Just get to that tower."

Chapter 21

Jesse opened his eyes slowly. The sky above was still gray, still smeared with soot, but something had changed. The haze had deepened, settled low, and a thin mist hung in the air. He blinked against it, confused for half a second, then felt a cold drop hit the back of his neck and trail down his collar.

Another drop landed on his cheek, then his brow, then the bridge of his nose. Rain, actual rain, sifting down from above in tiny, deliberate bursts. He lay there in the shallow draw letting the droplets find him. They hit his shirt and hissed against the heat still radiating from his skin. The soil around him began to darken. He opened his mouth and let one fall directly onto his tongue. It tasted like smoke and copper.

He didn't realize he was crying until he felt the warm tears mix with the cold water. The sensation confused him — wet and wet, one above, one below. His breath hitched, then steadied. He rolled to one elbow and pushed himself upright. The rain picked up as he moved, transitioning from scattered drops to a soft, steady patter that echoed through the skeletal forest like a whisper returning to life.

He turned his face upward and let the water wash the ash from his eyelids, from the corners of his cracked lips, and from the scars on his cheeks. His skin burned under the rinse, but it was a good burn. He unbuckled the straps on his pack and opened it to let the water soak the inner liner. It wasn't the most brilliant move, but he needed clean moisture. He needed to rinse his canteen and refill any containers that might hold liquid. He held out the empty bean can and let it fill, drop by drop, while he searched the nearby slope for a shallow depression that might pool.

The land responded. Within ten minutes, the rain found channels. Water trickled down the slope in thin, silver ribbons. Jesse followed one of them to a rock basin near a dead stump and used the knife to dig out a cleaner channel for flow. He rinsed his hands first, then his face, then poured a capful into his mouth and swished it, spitting twice before finally drinking. The water was cold. It was smoky but at the same time, it was perfect. He drank more before filling his canteen.

His foot still ached, the stitches pulsing under the pressure of movement, but the throb had dulled. The swelling had receded slightly. And most importantly, he was no longer walking in fear of collapse. The rain did that. It didn't solve everything. But it shifted the fight.

He sat for a while on a log, watching the droplets trace black streaks into the ash. He closed his eyes and tilted his head back, letting the rain hit his face. But the longer he sat, the more the pull returned. A quiet awareness: the rain wouldn't last forever, and this window — this brief, wet mercy — might be the safest passage he'd get.

"Keep moving while it's raining," he murmured.

Not because he wanted to. But because it was the smart play. Because water was cover. Because he could finally walk without fearing fire behind every rise. He stood, tested his balance, and gave the forest one last look before turning toward the slope.

* * *

191

The trail didn't reveal itself all at once. It began with a rhythm — not in sound, but in the way the land shifted beneath his boots. The slope eased into a flatter plane, and the trees, though burned to charcoal, grew in more uniform spacing. Jesse didn't recognize it immediately. The rain was still falling in soft, persistent sheets, plastering his hair to his scalp and dripping into his eyes, and he was more focused on where to place his injured foot next than on the bigger picture.

But then he saw it — a row of rocks, too evenly spaced to be natural, poking from the mud like vertebrae. Each one bore faint marks. Some charred, some split from heat, but one had a smear of bright orange paint, half-melted but unmistakable. Jesse stopped in his tracks and blinked the rain from his lashes.

"Trail," he said, voice cracked but steady.

He crouched carefully beside the painted rock, ran his fingers over the scar of color, and felt something pull tight in his chest. This wasn't wild anymore. This was managed. He stood and looked around. Now he saw it — the faint path carved through the slope, a corridor between two ridgelines where underbrush had once been cleared and then fire-scorched after. It was wide enough for a human. Too narrow for a vehicle. But it curved gently the way marked trails did — following terrain, not resisting it.

A fire line. Old or recent, he couldn't tell. The fire had come through here, no question. But someone had built this route before the burn. Someone had walked it, flagged it, and planned it. That meant something important: this led somewhere. A crew camp, an access road — maybe the tower.

He limped forward, following the bend. His foot protested with every step, but it held. The rain softened the trail dust, turning the ash to paste, but he didn't care. The line was visible now. He reached a charred stump with two nails driven into the top — symmetrical, rusted, but still aligned. He almost missed the plastic tag stapled to the side, melted and warped but bearing one burned letter:

"S"

Sector marker. Possibly for suppression, perhaps trail crew shorthand. But unmistakably official. He pressed a palm to it. It was real. It was his way out. For the first time in what felt like days, he wasn't walking blind. He wasn't moving because he had to, or because he was running from fire, or because hallucinations whispered from the trees. He was moving with intent.

He was no longer looking for rescue. He was following a line.

He passed another marker — a nailed tin square hanging loosely from a tree, scorched at the edges, the number "4" barely legible through the melted soot. Then farther down, the remains of a ribbon — red, wind-tattered — fluttered slightly from a branch near a split boulder. More sector flags.

Then, just off the bend, half-collapsed but still upright: a wooden signpost, nailed to a pair of poles driven deep into the dirt. The wood was scorched on one side, warped and cracked, but the lettering remained — faint, hand-carved, and blackened at the edges:

"Camp Raven - 1.3 mi →"

Camp Raven. He knew the name — barely. He read about it in the manual. Not one of the big bases. A seasonal checkpoint, more of a refuel station than a full operations hub. But if it was still intact, even partially, it could mean shelter. It could have a radio, a map, maybe even people. He touched the post then turned in the direction it pointed and started forward. The fire hadn't broken him. Not yet. And now, the line was holding.

Chapter 22

The rain had softened the land, and for the first time in days, the smoke in the air seemed less suffocating. The haze still clung in streaks along the low valleys, but higher up, the sky was beginning to pale, the edges of the clouds lifting just enough to let a suggestion of morning through. Jesse trudged forward along the faint track, each step calculated. His foot ached with every shift in weight, the stitches pulsing beneath the damp gauze, but the pain had dulled to something familiar. The ridge crested ahead, trees thinning, and then—through a break in the slope—he saw it.

What first looked like just another tangle of burned-out timbers slowly resolved into something with shape, with geometry. The roofline slanted at a clear angle, rusted metal sheets still clinging to part of the frame. A heavy beam stretched across two squat stone pillars, both blackened by fire but still upright. The front porch had collapsed under fallen branches and debris, half-buried in mud and ash, but the structure behind it held firm.

What stood there, defiant in ruin, was a ranger station. Or what remained of one. Jesse stopped in his tracks, heart knocking against his ribs. Slowly, he lifted his gaze. Up beyond the slope, above the tree line, half-shrouded by mist and clinging rain, a narrow silhouette cut against the brightening sky. A tower. Steel-legged, rusted, barely visible—but there. The same tower he had seen from the distant ridge near the cabin. He hadn't imagined it. This was it. This was Camp Raven.

He slowed, raising one hand to brace himself against a nearby trunk as he took it in. His grip on the walking stick tightened. His pulse lifted in his chest. He scanned the building for movement, for any hint that someone might be inside, but the forest remained hushed except for the dripping of rain through scorched eaves.

The steps had long since burned away, so he approached from the side, edging carefully around the heap of debris and hauling himself up onto what was left of the landing. The wood creaked under his weight but held. He moved along the wall, boots tracking ash and grit, until he reached the open doorway. The door itself had either burned or been removed, leaving a blackened threshold that yawned into darkness.

He leaned inside. The air was thick with the remnants of smoke and wet soot. A chemical tinge lingered beneath it—fire-retardant foam, maybe, or melted plastic. The interior was a skeleton of its former self. Beams sagged across the ceiling where they hadn't collapsed entirely. Shelves had been reduced to half-frames or piles of splinters. A desk near the back wall had been blackened on one side, the legs barely holding. Windowpanes were shattered or melted into drooping curves of glass. In the far corner, a bunk frame stood tilted, its mattress reduced to coiled springs and scraps of cloth. Nothing in here spoke of comfort.

But Jesse wasn't looking for that. He moved slowly, scanning the room for anything useful—supplies, gear, something with a power source. Then, just behind the scorched desk, he saw it. A radio. It was old—clearly pre-digital—bolted to the wall on a steel mounting bracket, its casing blistered from heat but miraculously intact. A coiled mic cord drooped beside it like a loop of wire, the handset resting in the debris at its base. He stared at it. Rain trickled through a hole in the ceiling and streaked the front panel, smearing soot across the dials. But the controls were still there.

He stepped forward, carefully avoiding the worst of the sagging floor. He crouched beside the desk and picked up the microphone, brushing dirt and grime from the push button with the edge of his thumb. The plastic felt cold, rough from the heat damage, but solid. He held it close and pressed the button.

"This is Jesse Brooks," he said, his voice hoarse from days without proper rest or water. "Volunteer fire crew, Bravo. If anyone can hear this..." His throat caught, breath trembling. "I'm alive."

He released the button. The room fell back into silence. He adjusted the dial one notch to the right and tried again. "This is Jesse Brooks. Fire line volunteer. I've been off-grid since the jump. If this station is still routing signals, if anyone's listening, please respond."

The speaker crackled. A faint hiss rose, static pushing weakly against the silence. He leaned in. Then, suddenly, a click. Brief. Barely a sound at all—but unmistakable. His pulse spiked. The speaker hissed louder. Then, through the noise, a fractured voice cut through. "…copy that. Say again, Jesse? Repeat. Did you say 'alive'?"

Jesse blinked, stunned by the sound of a human voice cutting across all that distance. His breath hitched in disbelief. Then a quiet laugh slipped from his throat —barely more than an exhale. "Yes," he whispered. "I'm alive."

The voice returned, clearer this time. "Repeat your position if you can. Are you mobile?"

It was a man's voice. Mid-forties, maybe. Calm, but marked by that edge of surprise that always came when someone expected silence and got something else. Jesse gripped the mic tighter and steadied his tone.

"I'm at Camp Raven," he said. "The ranger station. Or what's left of it. Structure's holding. I found the fire line and followed the markers. The radio still works—I don't know how, but it does."

There was a long pause. Keys clicked faintly in the background, paper shuffled.

"You're outside the last known containment arc," the voice finally replied. "We lost all signal in that area four days ago. Everyone assumed Raven burned."

"It almost did," Jesse said. "But I'm still here."

He leaned his back against the scorched wall, letting the rough texture press into his shoulders. Rain ran down his face in cold rivulets. The exhaustion hit harder now, crawling through his limbs in waves. With the adrenaline draining, the ache returned, deep and full. His stitched foot throbbed in rhythm with his heart.

"We've got your transmission," the voice said again. "We're locking coordinates now. Do you have visual markers? Smoke plumes? Chopper activity?"

"No chopper sounds," Jesse said. "No active smoke. The fire already passed through. I haven't seen anything moving for hours."

Another pause.

"We're bouncing your signal through the east ridge repeater. Weak, but holding. Stay on this channel. We're notifying Basecamp. Recovery's en route."

Jesse let the words settle in. They were sending someone. Someone knew he was alive.

He pressed the mic again. "Thank you," he said quietly. "You have no idea."

"You'd be surprised," came the reply.

There was a short silence, then the voice returned. "We're dispatching a chopper to your sector. Thirty to forty minutes for visual sweep. Do you have flares?"

Jesse glanced around. "No flares. No signal mirror. There's nothing here."

"We'll find you," the voice replied. "Get above the tree line if you can. Make yourself visible."

"I'll be ready," Jesse said, and let go of the mic.

He stared at the box for a long moment. Then he let himself slide down the wall to the floor. The wood was cold against his back. He folded his arms over his knees and rested his head there.

He didn't sleep. Not fully. Just let himself stop moving. The stillness didn't last. After a few minutes, he forced himself upright again. He couldn't let his body slip too far. Sleep could still turn dangerous. He limped to a busted drawer near the wall, found a bundle of white cloth stuffed inside, and tied it to a rusted antenna mount.

He took stock of his body. His foot was swollen but held. The bandage had slipped slightly during the climb to the station. Mud had dried near the sutures, but when he unwrapped it, the stitches still looked tight. He cleaned it with what cloth he had left, then wound a new strip around the sole. It wasn't medical-grade. But it would last.

He moved through the room, searching every corner. Near the old bunk frame, half buried in ash, he found a small tin box. Inside were three matchsticks, a rusted compass, and a photograph folded into quarters.

He opened it carefully. Three people stared out from the image—two men in crew shirts, one woman in a ranger's uniform. Their arms wrapped over shoulders, their faces bright despite the sun. Behind them, a controlled burn line crept along a distant slope. The fire was tame. He studied the photo for a long time. He didn't recognize them. But he understood them.

He folded the image and slid it into his jacket pocket. Then he returned to the desk and sat down again, stretching his injured foot out in front of him. His hand rested lightly on the microphone, though he didn't press it. Outside, the forest was quiet now, not from threat, but from rest. And for the first time in days, Jesse felt like he was waiting for something he believed would come.

Chapter 23

The sound reached Jesse like a memory returning. Faint at first, barely audible over the mist-softened quiet, it crept in as a low throb pressing against the distant hills. He froze in the doorway of the ruined ranger station, uncertain whether he was hearing something real or just another echo of hope playing tricks on his mind. But the pulse was steady. Mechanical. A rhythm unlike wind or water. It built slowly, a distinct repetition that set his nerves humming before he could name it.

He stepped forward, moving stiffly across the broken floorboards, every joint protesting. His body felt heavier with each minute of waiting, each second of silence. But now the quiet had shifted. He could feel it. That deep thrum didn't fade. It strengthened.

By the time he stepped into the clearing behind the station, the sound had become a presence—pounding through the air like a distant heartbeat. The rain had thinned to mist. His fingers trembled as he scanned the cloud-thick horizon. And then he saw it: the blurred silhouette of a helicopter cresting the ridge, dark and solid against the gray sky. It banked slowly, blades churning the fog, sweeping low over the trees. A real aircraft. A crew. A way out.

Jesse moved without thinking. He dragged himself across the clearing, stitches pulling, ankle screaming with every uneven step. He fought to keep his balance on the slick ash, the broken branch he'd used as a crutch digging into the mud with each lurch. With his other arm, he raised the antenna with the white cloth and waved it in wide arcs overhead, trying to draw their attention. His voice was gone. Worn to nothing over the days of shouting and smoke. There would be no calls, no cries. Just movement.

The chopper curved, dipped lower. The rhythm of its rotors pounded against his chest. It was working. They'd seen him. The wind came next—blasting through the clearing as the aircraft hovered overhead.

Rotor wash flattened the blackened underbrush and sent spirals of ash spinning like torn cloth. Jesse shielded his face with his arm, eyes squeezed shut against the sting of grit. The noise became overwhelming.

From the open side door, a crew member descended. Boots hit the ash-heavy soil in long, purposeful strides. The figure moved quickly, arms signaling to the crew still inside.

"Jesse Brooks?" the voice shouted, sharp over the roar.

Jesse raised his hand, chest heaving. He couldn't speak. His throat locked with exhaustion, but he nodded, firm and deliberate. The crew member was on him in seconds, one arm catching him under the shoulder. Jesse leaned in, letting the strength guide him up to the chopper. Another pair of hands reached from the cabin above, gripping his wrist and hauling him inside. The crutch fell to the dirt below, lost in the swirl.

The door slammed closed. The world changed again. Inside the cabin, everything was loud but contained. No wind, no ash, no weight of sky pressing down. Just the drumming of rotors, the clatter of harness buckles, and the low murmur of radio chatter. Jesse was guided into a seat and strapped in. His limbs hung heavy. His hands wouldn't stop shaking, but he gripped the belt across his chest as though it might vanish. A water bottle was pressed into his palm. He took it, unscrewed the cap, and drank with small, mechanical swallows. Cold water slid down his throat and made his whole body shudder. His lungs pulled air, but it felt like they were relearning how.

The helicopter gained altitude, banking slightly to clear the ridge, and through the window, Jesse watched the terrain fall away. Trees receded into dark smudges. Fire lines etched the hills like faint scars, curving through the wreckage. Far below, he could still see the twisted silhouette of Camp Raven's collapsed porch and shattered roof.

He stayed there, pressed to the window, taking in every shape, every slope, every burned seam. Not to memorize it. He already knew it all by heart. He was bearing witness. To what he'd survived. To what the fire had taken—and what it hadn't.

The seat beside him shifted. Another figure dropped into the chair—a man in his fifties, broad-shouldered, with ash-streaked gear and a headset pulled low. He didn't speak immediately. Just looked Jesse over, taking in the matted hair, the blackened skin, the sweat-streaked jacket, the boots caked with mud and blood.

"You're the one they thought was dead," the man said finally, voice low through the mic.

Jesse turned toward him, blinking hard. "I was," he said, barely more than a breath.

The man nodded slowly, like that was enough. They didn't speak for a while. The helicopter tilted slightly in a crosswind, then evened out. Sunlight began to break through the thinning haze in angled beams. The forest below gleamed in places—black turned to silver under the moving light.

The man leaned forward a bit, adjusting the comm. "We'll have you at Basecamp in under an hour. They've got medics standing by."

Jesse didn't respond. He wasn't thinking about Basecamp. Or medics. Or what happened next. His thoughts were still back there—in the station, in the trail leading to it, the slow unraveling of fear that came when a voice answered the radio. He closed his eyes briefly, listening to the hum of the engine, the beat of the blades, the shifting weight of the air.

Then, when he opened them again, the man beside him spoke one last time. "You survived something most wouldn't."

Jesse didn't answer. He wanted to, but his voice stayed quiet. Instead, he let the silence settle. Let the weight of rescue wrap around him like a blanket he didn't know he needed. The mountains fell behind them. And the path ahead was open.

Chapter 24

The hospital lights were too white. Not just bright, but unnatural. They hummed faintly overhead, flickering just enough to draw attention without fully breaking. Jesse stared up at them from the narrow bed, arms resting limp over the thin blanket, the pulse monitor chirping beside him like a distant metronome. Somewhere nearby, a cart squeaked. Rubber soles passed the door. Voices murmured in and out of earshot — nurses, maybe family members in the next room over.

The sounds felt fake. Like someone had left a television playing a hospital drama in another room, and he'd wandered too far inside it. He didn't belong here. He still smelled of ash, even after the scrubbing, even after the dressings and the clean sheets and the IV drip full of clear, cold fluid. They'd cleaned the outside. The inside hadn't caught up yet.

His foot was bandaged, stitched professionally now, not with bloodstained bootlace. His ribs were taped. His shoulder, the one that had taken the worst of the tumble near the creek bed, throbbed dully beneath a numbing agent they'd pushed a few hours ago. But all of that pain, all of that realness, still felt less immediate than the way the silence pressed on him.

They'd brought him in like he mattered. Medics waiting. A gurney. Oxygen. Cameras at the landing pad, though no one said anything about them. He remembered flashes of motion — someone shouting his name, a pair of gloved hands tapping his cheeks, asking him to stay awake. A blanket. Applause in the distance, maybe? That part felt wrong. It blurred into the buzz of the rotors and the sky lifting away. He hadn't spoken much since. He didn't feel the need. What was there to say?

A soft knock tapped on the door. He turned his head and saw a face in the gap. His mother. She hesitated before entering, one hand clutching her jacket tight at the collar like it might hold her together. Her eyes were swollen, but she wasn't crying. She looked like she already had, hard and long, and was now empty of everything but awe. Behind her stood his sister, smaller, hunched under the weight of the moment, and just behind them, his stepfather. No one said anything at first. The room was too still. Like everyone was afraid that if they moved too quickly, Jesse might vanish.

Finally, he said it first. "Hey."

The word came dry, barely more than breath, but it was enough to crack the standoff. His mother crossed the room and hugged him, wrapping her arms around his shoulders, her cheek brushing against his hair.

"You're home," she whispered. It wasn't a declaration. It was a plea.

Jesse didn't say anything in return. He no longer had the vocabulary for what *home* meant.

She pulled back, brushing a hand along the side of his face, her touch feather-light.

"Do you know how long it was?" Her voice cracked. "Eleven days. Jesse... we didn't know if—" She stopped herself, swallowed hard, then just shook her head.

"I wasn't far," Jesse murmured. A lie, but one that made her close her eyes and nod.

Eleven days. He let the number settle in his chest, heavier than it had any right to be. He hadn't been counting. Not really. Nights blurred. Days folded in on themselves. He remembered moments—heat, pain, hunger—but not time. Eleven days out there. It didn't feel real. But somehow, it was.

His sister moved closer next, reaching for his hand. He noticed she didn't look directly at his face. Her eyes hovered near his chest, his IV line, his hospital bracelet.

"You look…" her voice trailed off.

He raised an eyebrow. "Like hell?"

She snorted, a tear slipping sideways. "Yeah. Like hell."

His stepfather nodded to him across the bed, not with the awkward silence of a stranger, but with the muted respect of someone who didn't know how to comfort the living when they'd already begun mourning them.

"The station's been checking in," he said. "Everyone's been asking about you. Chief Mallory wants to come by as soon as they'll let him in."

Jesse looked down at his bandaged hands. They'd scrubbed the soot from under his nails, but his skin still looked gray around the knuckles, stained in the creases.

"I'm not sure I want them to," he said.

"They want to thank you," his stepfather said.

Jesse shook his head slowly. "I didn't save anybody."

"You saved *yourself*," his mother said, her voice firmer now. "That's not small."

Jesse didn't respond. He just nodded and closed his eyes again.

* * *

Later that evening, after the initial rush of visitors slowed, after the nurse came in with broth and pills and dimmed the lights halfway, Jesse stared out the hospital window at the small-town skyline — a water tower, some rooftop HVAC units, a neon sign blinking in amber at the corner of a strip mall.

He used to know every streetlight in this town. Could bike from the firehouse to his mom's in under seven minutes. Knew which hill got the sunrise first and which alley behind the diner always smelled like grease, no matter how often they washed it down. Now, looking out over it, everything felt flatter. Smaller, as if he were seeing it through glass.

There was a knock, then the door creaked open. Chief Mallory stepped inside, his helmet tucked under one arm, his boots leaving scuffs of dust on the tile. He didn't speak right away, just gave Jesse a nod, the kind that carried more weight than a hundred words.

"The nurses said I could have five minutes," he said, keeping his voice low. "Hope that's all right."

Jesse nodded. "Yeah. It's fine."

Mallory moved to the chair by the bed but didn't sit. He looked at Jesse for a long moment. "You gave us a scare," he said. "We had crews combing half the county. Air teams, trackers, volunteer search lines. Every time the smoke shifted, we thought we'd lost our window."

"I didn't know anyone was looking," Jesse said. His voice cracked more than he wanted it to.

"Well," Mallory said gently, "we were."

Silence settled between them. Jesse stared at the IV line in his arm. Mallory rested his helmet on the edge of the windowsill.

"You did everything we trained you to do," Mallory added. "More than that. You adapted. You kept moving. You didn't give up."

"I made mistakes," Jesse said, the words falling out before he could stop them. "I broke protocol. I lost the line. I—"

"You survived," Mallory cut in. His tone wasn't harsh, but it left no room for argument. "You were in a live scenario no one expected to go south. And you're sitting here now because you didn't panic. That counts."

Jesse let the words hang in the air. He wanted to believe them.

Mallory straightened, helmet in hand again. "I'll let you rest," he said. "But I meant it, Jesse — the department's proud of you. I'm proud of you."

He paused at the door. "Doesn't matter how far you got from the crew. You found your way back."

Jesse didn't know what to say. So he just nodded. Mallory gave him one last look and slipped out into the hall. The room was quiet again. But Jesse's chest felt different. Like something had clicked into place.

Maybe not peace. But something close.

Chapter 25

The discharge took less time than expected. Just a nurse with a clipboard, a printed packet of wound care instructions, and a reminder to hydrate. His mom signed a form while he laced up one boot, the other foot still too swollen for anything but a hospital slide-on and a wrap.

They wheeled him to the lobby. As the elevator doors opened, Jesse spotted a small group waiting near the glass entrance. And his stomach went tight. There was more than just family. Two uniformed firefighters stood by the door — not from his unit, but from a nearby station. One of them was holding a folded T-shirt with the station's logo on the chest. Behind them, a woman in a blazer clutched a small notepad, a pen already uncapped in her hand. Near the curb, a parked county van idled with its hazard lights on.

The nurse gave a quick smile and said, "Looks like you've got a welcome party."

Outside, sunlight washed everything in false warmth. There was a banner tied between two parking signs that read WELCOME BACK JESSE in black marker. Two kids were holding handmade signs. One said, "YOU'RE A HERO." The other had flames drawn on it, red and orange crayons. He blinked at that one. Flames.

He stood awkwardly at the edge of the sidewalk while his mother thanked everyone for coming. His sister stood beside him, looping an arm through his like she thought he might fall. He wouldn't. Not physically. But something inside was already tipping.

The woman in the blazer stepped forward. "Mr. Brooks?" she asked, smiling with practiced warmth. "County communications. We've had several outlets reach out — nothing formal right now, but we'd love a quote, maybe a short video for the department's social channels."

He squinted at her. "A video?"

"Just a thank-you message. You know, something hopeful. People are calling you the Lucky Line Walker." She laughed, like it was a joke.

Jesse didn't laugh.

"I didn't walk a line," he said, his voice flat. "Not really."

She shifted her weight, still smiling, but with a nervous edge now. "Of course, of course. Just a name someone came up with on the news."

He nodded once and turned away from her without another word.

They loaded into the county van. He sat by the window, arms crossed loosely over his chest, head resting on the glass. They took the long route through town — on purpose, he realized — so that people could wave. And they did.

Outside the window, people clapped. A few saluted. He closed his eyes. He wanted to vanish. The town had built a version of him in his absence — brave, sure-footed, fire-tested. A myth, crafted from rumor and fragments of radio chatter. They needed a story, and he was the one still breathing.

But the Jesse they were cheering for didn't exist. That Jesse didn't fall apart halfway through the second night. That Jesse didn't hallucinate his father's voice whispering to him out of the trees.

He wanted to tell them that heroes don't cry in the dirt, begging shadows for answers. That heroes don't eat ants because there's nothing else. That heroes don't hear silence so deep it presses down on your ribs until it feels like drowning. But those weren't the parts anyone wanted to hear. They wanted the photo. The patch. The clean ending. The truth didn't fit on a banner.

When they pulled up to his mother's house, neighbors were already waiting — a few holding paper plates of brownies, others just standing there, smiling widely.

The moment he stepped out of the van, someone called, "Welcome home, Jesse!"

He raised a hand in thanks. It felt like it belonged to someone else. A woman he didn't recognize hugged him. A man slapped him on the back. His mother tried to shoo them back gently, saying he needed rest, that he wasn't ready for a crowd. Jesse didn't argue. He didn't speak much at all. He let them have their moment. And then he slipped inside.

The living room was exactly how he remembered it. Couch a little crooked. TV remote missing its back panel. A framed photo on the shelf showing him in his cadet uniform from two years ago, beaming, the sun too bright in the shot. He stared at it for a long time. He didn't know that kid anymore.

That night, he sat on the back steps alone, watching the sky. The air smelled of barbecue from a few houses over. Someone was laughing too loudly. A sprinkler clicked on across the street. He hadn't heard sprinklers in weeks.

His hands rested loosely on his knees. Still scabbed and stiff. He felt more like himself out here in the quiet. But even this didn't feel like *his* life. It felt like the ghost of it. A version left behind when the fire came. When his mom poked her head out and asked if he was hungry, he just shook his head.

"Maybe later," he replied.

She nodded like she understood. But he wasn't sure he'd ever be hungry again in the same way.

* * *

The next day, he took a walk to the firehouse. It looked smaller than he remembered. Not by much — just enough to feel off. The bay doors were up, the red trucks gleaming in the sun like they'd been washed that morning. The same white hose rack. Same tan-and-yellow gear lined up along the wall, helmets tilted forward on hooks like heads bowed in silent attention. Nothing had changed. And that was the hardest part.

Jesse stood just outside the threshold, his hand hovering near the doorframe. He'd spent the better part of a year here — shadowing calls, scrubbing gear, learning from the full-timers and seasoned volunteers. His father had worked here once, long before the accident, and that legacy had opened the door for Jesse. It was where he'd first pulled hose, first practiced CPR, first heard his name called out over the station speaker. It was why he'd gotten into the wildfire training program in the first place.

His boots were clean now. The bandages on his hands were fresh. But his shadow still stretched long across the cement floor, and it didn't feel like it belonged to him.

Captain Shaw spotted him first. She stood near the back wall, clipboard in one hand, a half-filled coffee mug in the other. She'd always been sharp — eyes that missed nothing, a voice that could command a room with a single syllable. But now, seeing him, her face softened.

"Brooks," she said, setting down the mug.

He nodded. "Ma'am."

She crossed the room in quick, even steps. For a moment, it looked like she might hug him, then thought better of it. Instead, she placed a hand on his shoulder and gave a firm squeeze. "Glad to have you back."

He didn't know how to answer that, so he just said, "Thanks."

The rest of the crew emerged slowly from the side hallway — some from the kitchen, others from the back office. A few he knew well, others only by nickname and station number. Murmured greetings followed, and claps on the shoulder. One of them held out a fresh crew patch — clean, ironed flat.

"Replacement," the guy said with a grin. "We figured yours got a little crispy."

Jesse managed a half smile. "Yeah. Something like that."

They gathered in the break room. Someone handed him a bottle of soda. Another pushed over a folding chair, and Jesse sat slowly, stretching out his still-wrapped foot with care. The crew chatted like usual — some about a brush call from earlier in the week, one joking about a rookie backing the engine into a mailbox. Laughter broke out, light and familiar. And Jesse watched it all from the outside. Even seated in the middle of the room, he felt peripheral — like static in a clear frequency.

Captain Shaw sat down beside him. "You don't have to stay long," she said gently. "We just wanted to see you. Let you know the door's open when you're ready."

He stared at the tabletop for a long second.

"Feels weird," he said finally. "Being back."

"I'd be more concerned if it didn't," she replied.

Jesse glanced sideways at her. "I didn't do anything special."

"You survived something that should've killed you," she said. "That counts."

"I didn't follow protocol. I broke from the group. Lost the radio. Got turned around. I was—" He stopped, jaw tightening.

"I wasn't strong," he continued. "I was lucky."

Captain Shaw leaned back slightly, arms crossed. "Let me tell you something, Brooks. Every survivor I've ever met says the same thing. That they didn't earn it. That they made mistakes. That it was chance, or fate, or something dumb like a shift in the wind."

She nodded toward the patch still clutched in his hand. "But they came back. And that's the difference."

He looked down at the patch. Ran a thumb along the stitching. He wasn't sure he wanted to wear it again. Not yet. Maybe not ever.

Before he left, they took a group photo. He smiled for it. Not because he felt it, but because he knew that's what people needed. When he walked out, the bay doors were still up. The light was sharper now. The sky a deeper kind of blue. It was the same place. The same house. The one that trained him, challenged him, trusted him. But it didn't feel like his house anymore. He wasn't sure it ever would again.

Chapter 26

The cemetery sat at the edge of town, tucked between a slope of dried field grass and a low ridge that caught the wind just enough to rattle the dry leaves clinging to a line of poplars. Jesse hadn't been there since the funeral. Back then, the dirt around the stone had been freshly turned, darker than the rest. Now, seasons had come and gone, and the grass had grown back thin and wild. The headstone had settled. The dirt had crusted. It looked permanent now.

He stepped through the creaking gate with a slow, deliberate limp. His foot still hadn't fully healed, and the uneven gravel path pressed through his boot sole like memory: persistent and uncomfortable. He didn't bother looking around. He knew where the grave was. Third row from the west fence. Middle stone, second from the cross marker.

He wasn't carrying flowers. He didn't think his father would've wanted them anyway. Instead, tucked in the inside pocket of his canvas jacket was a palm-sized piece of pine bark, charred lightly at the edges. He'd shaved the soot away from the center until it revealed the grain beneath — smooth, pale brown. Into that, he had carved two letters: **JB**. His. And his father's.

He had used a pocketknife that had been dulled halfway through. The work had taken a half hour, maybe more. He had done it at the edge of the woods behind his house, alone, sitting cross-legged in the dirt while his mother thought he was inside resting. He didn't known what else to bring.

The stone was as plain as ever. Gray, rectangular, etched with his father's full name and the firehouse emblem at the top. There were still scorch marks at the base — remnants of a burn that had passed through the ridge during a wind shift days after the burial. The fire hadn't taken the cemetery, but it had kissed the edge, singed the grass and streaked soot across half the markers.

He sat down carefully in front of it, folding one leg underneath him, the other stretched out. Sitting here, in the shadow of his father's stone, normal felt like a lie. He pulled the piece of bark from his pocket and held it in both hands. It wasn't much. Maybe it didn't need to be. His father had taught him that not everything had to say something to mean something. Some things just were.

He placed it at the base of the marker, leaning it against the stone, then brushed a little gravel away from the spot to keep it from sliding. For a long time, he said nothing.

Wind passed across the cemetery in soft waves, rustling the dry grass and clacking branches together. Somewhere far off, a lawnmower buzzed in a backyard nearby. The occasional bark of a dog cut through the silence like punctuation.

Jesse exhaled through his nose. "You didn't tell me it would be like that," he murmured. His voice was low. Not accusatory. Just… there.

"You told me about fear. About how it crawls up your spine when the wind shifts. About heat. Smoke. The way your hands shake after a rescue, even if you don't remember them shaking during. But you never talked about being alone."

He looked down at his own fingers. They were clean. Pink again. The blisters were healing. His nails had grown back. There was no trace of the dirt he'd clawed through.

"I didn't know it would get that quiet," he said. "That still. Like the world had gone out and I forgot to follow."

He tilted his head back and stared up at the bare sky.

"You always said fire doesn't play favorites. That it doesn't care how brave you are, or how long you've served, or how many drills you ran last week. And you were right. I just didn't think I'd come back from it."

There was no answer, of course. No gust of wind at just the right time. No voice in his head. No warmth on his back. He didn't believe in that. But he believed in memory. And memory had a voice.

He remembered his father's hands — broad, weathered, always dry. The way he'd rest one of them on Jesse's shoulder whenever he gave advice, grounding the words with weight. Not for comfort. For anchor. His father never said things he didn't mean, and when he did speak, it was usually with the kind of clarity that cut through noise. So Jesse imagined what he'd say now. And it wasn't praise.

It wasn't "You did good."

It was probably more like, "You learned something, didn't you?"

He leaned forward slightly, resting his elbows on his knees. His body still ached in dull, persistent ways. The cold in the earth beneath him seeped slowly upward into his spine, his ribs, his hip. He didn't move.

"I don't know if I'm going back," he said. "I thought I would. Before. When I was still out there. That was the goal, you know? Get out. Get home. Get back on the truck. Prove it didn't break me."

He ran a hand down his face and shook his head slowly. "But I don't know if it didn't. I feel like... I left something out there. Or maybe something out there took something I didn't know I had."

The wind shifted slightly, and a branch overhead creaked. He reached out and straightened the piece of bark again where it had leaned too far.

"I think if you were here, you'd tell me that was okay," he added. "That not everything has to go back to the way it was."

He swallowed once, throat tight.

"You'd tell me that sometimes the only way forward is through."

He looked at the initials carved into the bark. Not much, really. But it felt like a signature. Not just on this stone, but on everything that had come before it. He stayed there a long time. Longer than he meant to. Until the clouds began to gather, soft and silver, and the edge of dusk started creeping into the air. The lawnmower sounds had faded. The dog had stopped barking.

The cemetery was just a hill again. A place for endings. And Jesse wasn't sure anymore if he'd come here for closure or for permission. Either way, he'd gotten what he needed. He stood slowly, bracing himself against the stone with one hand. The wind tugged gently at the hem of his jacket. His breath clouded as he turned toward the gate. He didn't look back.

The path down felt shorter than it had on the way up, like the hill had let go of something. At the gate, he rested his hand on the post, just for a second. There was no ceremony to the moment, no final thought to mark it. Just a quiet understanding. He walked on, not to forget, but because it was time. Some part of him — the part that had been stuck there for years — finally knew how to leave.

Epilogue

Jesse stood at the edge of the training camp with his boots planted in the same packed dirt where he'd stood twelve months ago — only this time, it wasn't nerves tying his gut into knots. It was something calmer. Weight, maybe. Or perspective.

Pine Pass hadn't changed much. The trucks still idled with the same diesel cough. The gear shed still leaned slightly to one side. And the cook, Roy, was already hollering about breakfast portions from behind the mess window. Somewhere beyond the treeline, ravens cackled in the hot morning air.

He adjusted his radio strap, tightening it across his shoulder. His foot had long since healed, though some mornings it still ached, especially when rain was coming. He didn't mind. It was part of him now.

Ortiz was leaning against the hood of the engine, sipping coffee that probably hadn't been hot since sunrise. "You look taller," he said without looking up. "That happen, or am I just shrinking?"

Jesse smirked. "Could be both."

"You back to stay this time?" a voice asked behind him.

Jesse turned to see Riley with the same scowl softened by experience. But his eyes didn't hold skepticism anymore. They held something closer to respect. Maybe even trust.

"I'm not going anywhere," Jesse said.

"Try not to get lost this time," Riley said, deadpan as ever.

Jesse turned, eyebrow raised. "No promises," he said. "But I brought a better map."

Ortiz let out a sharp laugh as he adjusted his pack. "Good, 'cause if you vanish again, I'm not climbing halfway across a ridge with smoke in my shorts to track you down. I'm old. My knees make sounds now."

"You're thirty-two," Ash muttered, stepping up beside Jesse.

"Exactly," Ortiz said, pointing at her. "That's ancient in fire years."

Jesse smiled and glanced at Ash. She met his look, then gave a short nod.

"No one thought you'd come back," she said.

Jesse shrugged. "I didn't know I would, either."

Chief Mallory emerged from the ops tent with a clipboard under one arm and his radio squawking at his belt. His face was the same unreadable map of lines and fire-worn calm, but his eyes lit when they met Jesse's.

"You remember the way to Section D?" he asked.

"Yeah," Jesse said. "I remember everything."

Mallory handed him the clipboard. It wasn't symbolic. It was procedural. But Jesse felt the difference as he took it. Felt the quiet authority passed down in the smallest of gestures.

He tucked the clipboard under one arm and turned toward the rookies — six of them lined up awkwardly near the gear bins, each one stiff and trying to hide their nerves. Their hard hats gleamed like they'd never seen soot before. Jesse stepped forward.

"You three," he said, pointing to a group clustered near the edge, "grab pulaskis and join Ash at the ridgeline. She'll walk you through where we're thinning brush."

Then, to another recruit with nervous hands: "You're with me on drip torch. Ever used one?"

The kid shook his head.

"You will today. Stick close. Watch your spacing. If I say stop, stop."

Jesse caught a brief glance from Mallory, who gave a short nod and turned away — a quiet show of trust. He'd seen enough to know Jesse had it handled.

A breeze shifted through the clearing. Smoke from a small prep burn curled beyond the tree line, rising in lazy spirals. Jesse inhaled through his nose, tasting cedar and carbon.

Ortiz clapped him once on the shoulder. "Feels good, doesn't it?"

"Yeah," Jesse said. "It does."

He turned toward the crew. The line would be cut soon. The terrain was nearly prepped. One hand dropped to the fusee at his belt. He raised his voice just enough to carry. "Alright, guys," he said. "Let's light up the burn line."

About the author:

Adam McKim was born and raised in a small town in Missouri, where he still lives today with his wife and son. He began writing in his early twenties and has authored a growing collection of poems and books. When he's not writing, he enjoys quiet moments with family and the continued pursuit of storytelling.